"I suppose you'll be eating with the Starks."

"Yes, we will."

"Why do you bother pretending?"

Deborah stared at Lenore. "Pretending what?"

Lenore shrugged. "You and Dane. It's so obvious, everyone knows."

Deborah's hand rested on her stomach. Had she been fooling herself? Cora had noticed, but surely no one else had. Dane still didn't know about the baby.

When she didn't respond, Lenore shook her head. "That kiss. Your marriage. It's all a big deception, isn't it? You can't honestly believe anyone thinks you have a real marriage. You don't even sleep in the same room."

The hot flush of anger swept over Deborah. "What business is it of yours whether our marriage is real or not?"

Lenore shifted Beth to the side. "Because, Dane loves me."

MILDRED COLVIN is a native Missourian with three children, one son-in-law, and three grandchildren. She and her husband spent most of their married life providing a home for foster children but now enjoy babysitting the grandchildren. Mildred writes inspirational romance because in them the truth of God's presence, even in the midst of trouble, can be portrayed. Her desire is to continue writing stories that uplift and encourage.

Books by Mildred Colvin

HEARTSONG PRESENTS

Don't miss out on any of our super romances. Write to us at the following address for information on our newest releases and club information.

Heartsong Presents Readers' Service
PO Box 721
Uhrichsville, OH 44683

Or visit www.heartsongpresents.com

Deborah

Mildred Colvin

Heartsong Presents

To those who read and enjoy my books. Without you, there would be no reason to write. May God's blessings always be yours.

Also to my son, Jonathan, who once upon a time was an adorable two-year-old much like Tommy Stark. Now he's a man with his own family. Always walk with God, Jon.

A note from the Author:
I love to hear from my readers! You may correspond with me by writing:

Mildred Colvin
Author Relations
PO Box 721
Uhrichsville, OH 44683

ISBN 978-1-59789-394-7

DEBORAH

All scripture quotations are taken from the King James Version of the Bible.

Our mission is to publish and distribute inspirational products offering exceptional value and biblical encouragement to the masses.

PRINTED IN THE U.S.A.

one

St. Louis, 1865

Deborah Asberry stood by the open grave between her mother and younger brother. Her husband's body rested in a pine casket next to the gaping hole, waiting to be lowered into the earth.

Tears ran down her cheeks as her father's voice, often choked by grief, expounded the bravery and sacrifice of his much loved son-in-law who had given his life in service to his country.

"Struck down by a rebel bullet in the prime of life, Jamison Lee Asberry fought with valor to reunite this great land. We will not forget Jamison or will our love for him wane as we look forward to seeing him again in that Holy City one day where we shall ever be with the Lord."

You loved Jamison, Father, but I didn't. I shall grieve for the loss of a young life, but I cannot grieve for lost love when there was none. Deborah knew her thoughts would have shocked everyone there. Everyone except her brother, Caleb. He knew she had been forced to marry Jamison. He alone knew how much she had hated the very idea.

She mopped at the tears and felt her Caleb's arm slip around her shoulders. At sixteen, and four years younger than Deborah, he still stood a head above her. She leaned into his comforting embrace.

"It'll be all right, sis." His whispered words brought little assurance. "At least you don't have to live with him anymore."

"Father says I must move back home." Just the thought brought

5

a fresh surge of tears. She knew they shouldn't be whispering during the service, so she forced a smile for her brother. "I'm sure you are right, though. Everything will work out."

"Shall we pray?" Jacob Smith, Deborah's father and pastor of the country church that sat beside the cemetery, bowed his head. "Father, into Your hands we commit the spirit of this beloved son, husband, and friend. He was Your child, born again of the Spirit of God. Truly a man of God, he served You in all his ways."

Her father's voice droned on as Deborah determined to make the most of her situation. She wiped the remaining tears from her face, knowing that she had no choices in her life. If her father said she must move back home, that's what she would do. Already her belongings had been taken to her father's house.

Her married life, though quite short, had taken her out from under her father's rule for almost a month. She and Jamison were married in a simple ceremony conducted in the church by her father. For two weeks they had lived together in the small cottage three blocks from her childhood home. In those two weeks she had learned that life under her husband's rule differed little from life under her father's rule. Then Jamison returned to his unit, and Deborah became mistress of her own home. For twelve days she had lived the life of freedom in a land torn by war.

Deborah let out a ragged sigh. What difference did it make? Married or single, her life was not her own and never would be.

Jacob no sooner had closed his prayer than a yell of triumph broke the muted sounds of weeping. A rider on horseback galloped hard toward the cemetery. With scarcely a pause in step, he called as he rode past, "The war's over! The South has surrendered!"

As if caught by an invisible net held by the rider, men and women ran to their buggies and horses. Soon the road leading into town became alive in a race for truth.

"No—o—o." The word became a wail as Jamison's mother fell to her knees before the closed casket. Her sobs and keening touched Deborah's heart. To lose her only son within days of the surrender no doubt was more than she could bear.

Deborah knelt beside the older woman and placed her arm around her shoulders. Her husband knelt on the other side, tears streaming down his face.

"I'm so sorry." Deborah tried to lend comfort only to have her mother-in-law pull away.

"Come, Deborah." Her father grasped her arm. "We must be going."

She watched Jamison's father lead his grieving wife away. Neither spoke to Deborah. By the time she and her father climbed into their buggy, the workers had lowered the casket and began covering it with dirt. Deborah watched until her father drove the buggy out of the churchyard, and then she turned her back on her married life and her in-laws.

Her father stopped at the parsonage long enough for Deborah and her mother to climb down. Then he and Caleb joined the throng seeking confirmation of the word that had already spread like wildfire across St. Louis, Missouri, that the War Between the States had at last ended.

Taking advantage of the reprieve her father's absence gave, Deborah went upstairs to her room. She closed the door and sank to her old bed. One glance around her bedroom revealed the few pieces of furniture she had taken with her into marriage. Her wardrobe stood against the wall again with all her clothing in it, and her trunk sat at the end of her bed.

She had been glad to leave Jamison's clothing and all his belongings to his mother. What the woman might do with them, Deborah neither knew nor cared. She looked down at her left hand where her wedding ring still remained. The plain gold band gleamed in the light from her window. She moved to the window seat and leaned back against the inside wall.

Slipping the ring from her finger, she looked inside where the initials D.R.S. and J.L.A. had been engraved with a heart between. A tear slipped from her eye and another followed.

Why couldn't she have found someone to love who would love her as much? She closed her eyes and leaned her head back, letting her fingers curl around the ring.

"Lord, why? Does love between husband and wife exist? Now that the war is over the men will be coming home. Am I asking too much? Please forgive me if I am. But if there is love left in this world, could You please send someone to me who will love me and treat me and our children with gentleness and care?"

Deborah allowed the pain of her lost dreams to wash over her as she leaned against the wall. After several minutes, she lifted her spirit before her Lord in praise and submission. "I am sorry, Lord, that I have questioned Your will for my life. For surely You know all things. You know my coming in and my going out forever. I give my will to You. Please help me submit to my father's direction."

With renewed peace in her heart, Deborah stood and crossed to her dresser. She opened the top drawer and took out a small box that held special treasures from her girlhood. Dropping in her wedding ring to nestle with a broken necklace and her grandmother's cameo brooch, Deborah closed the lid, placed the box back in the drawer, and went downstairs.

She found her mother in the kitchen. "Have Father and Caleb returned?"

"I heard the buggy just before you came down." Her mother

crossed the kitchen and placed a hand on each of Deborah's shoulders as she searched her face. "Are you all right, dear?"

Deborah felt tears spring to her eyes at her mother's sympathy. She gave a short laugh that sounded more like a sob. "Oh Mother, I'm fine. I will grieve for Jamison because he died so young and so near the end of the war, but I will be fine."

The young widow brushed at the tears that would not stop. "But what will I do? I can't live in my father's house forever. I'm no longer a child."

" 'Take. . .no thought for the morrow.' " Her mother quoted the words of Christ, and Deborah knew she had been reprimanded in her mother's own gentle way. "Let's get through the next few days before we think of packing you off again, shall we?"

Deborah nodded, and the women separated to set out dishes of food that had been brought in by members of their church congregation.

❧

Within a few short days, Deborah realized she had already fallen into the old habits of her childhood. So short had her marriage been that she felt as if it were nothing more than a figment of her imagination. Then almost one week after Jamison's funeral, the world rocked with the shocking news that President Abraham Lincoln had been shot down while attending a theater with his wife. Deborah had yet to recover from the national tragedy when her father called the family into the parlor after church the following Sunday evening.

Deborah sensed tension between her parents as she sat perched on the edge of her chair. She had no doubt this meeting concerned her.

Jacob Smith sat in the center of the sofa, leaning forward with his elbows on his knees, his head bowed as if in prayer. His wife, like Deborah, sat forward in her chair, her back rigid and her face expressionless except for the worry in her eyes.

Caleb stood behind Deborah's chair as if he, too, knew the news would not be good.

Jacob lifted his head and spoke. "I have received a letter from a small country church in the southwest part of the state. They've asked me to conduct a revival meeting. Mrs. Cora Stark, the lady who wrote, is an old family friend. Years ago, when we were children here in St. Louis, we all played together—I with her younger brother and she and her sister with your Aunt Margaret."

Deborah watched her father, wondering what this had to do with her.

"Mrs. Stark moved with her family to that sparsely settled part of Missouri back in the thirties and met her husband there. I understand her husband, Mr. Aaron Stark, is a good Christian man, and together they have raised seven fine boys." Jacob cleared his throat before going on.

"In her letter, Mrs. Stark wrote of her oldest son, Dane." He looked down at his hands. "He recently lost his wife in childbirth and is bearing the burden of raising his two small children alone. Mrs. Stark has tried to get him to allow another member of the family to take the children until they are older, but he refuses."

Jacob met Deborah's puzzled gaze with a stern look. "It is quite admirable that this young man desires to to keep his children with him as they, too, have suffered greatly in the loss of their mother."

Deborah felt an icy tremor of premonition move through her body. She anticipated her father's next words before he spoke.

"Your mother and I have discussed this, and after much prayer I have decided that, considering your own recent loss, it would be prudent to accept this offer."

"Offer?" Deborah had not expected this so soon. "I don't

understand what you mean, Father."

Jacob's steel-gray eyes fixed on her as he answered. "Next week, Deborah, you and I are going to southern Missouri, where we will meet Mr. Dane Stark and determine if it is indeed God's will that you and he marry. If all seems well, you will become the wife of a fine Christian young man and a mother to his child and baby."

By whose standard will we determine if all is well, Father? Deborah didn't bother voicing her concern because she already knew the answer. For the second time in half a year, she would be forced to marry a man she didn't love and who did not love her. Only this time she would be torn from her mother and brother and might never see them again.

She turned to her mother for support but realized none would be coming as her mother sat with her head bowed, looking at neither husband nor daughter.

Deborah tried to reason with him. "But, Father, Jamison is scarcely cold in his grave. It isn't proper that I marry again so soon."

Jacob brushed her concern aside. "Recent events have brought many changes to our land, Deborah. The country is ripe for revival. Now is the time to go. Besides, you will be far from Jamison's family and friends. No one in southern Missouri will think ill of you."

"Father, what if Deborah doesn't want to go?" Caleb asked. His hand touched her shoulder.

"We will not discuss that. Certainly Deborah does not want to be remiss in her Christian duty to help a brother in need. She will benefit from this union as well, if this young man is indeed a born-again believer as his mother says. My telegram should have reached the Starks by now so all is settled."

Deborah's heart sank at her father's words. There would be no room for discussion. He had made up his mind. She barely listened as he talked about his plans. All she heard was that they would be leaving in two days which would give her scarcely enough time to pack her trunk.

Before she went to bed that night, Deborah sat on the window seat in her room and looked out at the stars shining in the black sky above. She had been born again at a young age. As long as she could remember, she had tried to live her life to please her father.

At his insistence, she had married Jamison, who was so much like her father he could have been his own son. She had hated the war, but when Jamison left she had secretly rejoiced. For the first time in her life she thought she would have a home of her own where no one berated her or told her what to do.

Now she would be forced to again marry against her will. She thought of the infant her father had mentioned and wondered if it was a girl or a boy. She had never held or cared for a baby and knew so little about them that the thought of motherhood frightened her. What if she did something wrong? Jamison had struck her only once in their short married life and not so very hard then. But what of this other man? Would he take his anger out on her with blows?

What had her mother said the day of Jamison's funeral? " 'Take. . .no thought for the morrow.' " Deborah quoted the words from Matthew 6:34 in her darkened room, bringing a measure of comfort. " 'Sufficient unto the day is the evil thereof,' " she added.

She slipped into bed to pray, turning her fears over to her heavenly Father.

two

Deborah clutched her handbag close against the sudden hiss and jerk of the train. She looked through the smoke-hazed window and wished her mother and brother could have come with them. But Father had barely given them time to say their good-byes at the house before he rushed her off to the train station. He didn't seem to care that she might never see her family again.

Stores and office buildings moved past the window slowly at first, then gathered speed as the train gained momentum. First residences and then farms and open fields replaced the city. Deborah watched the fields of grain become a blur in her vision.

She turned just enough to see her father. He did not pay her any mind, which suited Deborah. She preferred her own company.

As the morning wore away, Deborah longed to stand and stretch. They had passed through several villages, stopping only once for water. The passengers had been allowed a fifteen-minute break, which gave barely enough time to take a turn in the outhouse behind the way station and stretch a bit. That had been two hours ago.

Deborah's stomach rumbled. She placed her hand over the emptiness to will away the pangs of hunger. A loud whistle and a huge puff of black smoke announced their arrival in the town of Rolla. Deborah straightened, trying to see out her window that was now covered with smoke and soot. By the time the smoke cleared, the train had come to a shuddering stop.

"Come, Deborah." Her father stood, waiting for her to join

him before leading her down the long aisle toward the door. "This is where we get off."

Deborah stiffened as she followed her father. She would marry this man from the backwoods of southern Missouri, and she would make a home for herself where no man ruled her life. How she intended to do that by marrying another man of her father's choosing, she had no idea. But somehow, she promised herself, this time would be different. This time, far removed from her father's influence, she would stand up for herself and make a home she could call her own. She had to, because she would not get another chance.

"We'll take a stagecoach directly from here to Lebanon." Her father's words confirmed that her hunger would not be appeased anytime soon.

"How far will that be, Father?" she asked, dreading the answer.

"Why, not more than a sixty-mile distance. From there it will be almost straight west to our destination." He smiled down at her in a rare moment of consideration. "Take courage, child; your mother has prepared a bite to tide us over until we reach a station that serves hot meals."

Dusk covered the village of Lebanon by the time they rolled to a stop at the relay station. Deborah accepted her father's helping hand before climbing down from the stagecoach. Every bone in her body ached, every muscle screamed for rest. Never had she spent such a day. She had done nothing but sit, yet she felt as if she had worked long hours scrubbing on the washboard.

For the second time that day, her father smiled at her as they entered the inn where they would eat and rent rooms for the night. "Let's see what the cook has prepared for our supper. We scarcely ate at noon, and I daresay I'm quite hungry. How about you, Deborah?"

She looked at her father's smile then turned away and nodded. "Yes, I'm hungry, too."

Deborah sat at the table and smiled at a girl near her own age who placed filled plates in front of them. "Thank you."

"You are most welcome." The girl curtsied a quick dip and left. Turnips smothered with butter and baked beans in molasses covered one side of her plate. Thin slices of beef on thick slabs of bread covered the other side. Deborah wondered if she could eat it all. She could still feel the sway and jolt of the coach and felt little interest in the food in front of her despite her hunger. She lifted a fork loaded with baked beans to her mouth and almost sighed as the flavor aroused her appetite. By the time her father finished his supper her plate was also empty.

Several minutes later, Deborah slipped into her long, flannel nightgown and crawled into bed. As soon as her head touched the pillow she slept.

"Deborah!" Loud pounding on her door awakened her, and she jumped from bed confused. She could scarcely see in the dark room.

"Yes, Father, I'm awake." She opened the door just enough to see her father standing in the hall.

He seemed to be in a pleasant mood. "The Lord has graciously granted us transportation for the last leg of our journey. I've hired a hack that delivers mail three times a week. We'll have to change conveyances at each stop, but we must praise God for His provisions."

"Yes, Father," Deborah agreed, as she knew he would expect.

Jacob smiled. "Hurry now with your morning preparations. We cannot keep the mail service waiting."

Deborah turned from the door and lit the lamp sitting on a table by the bed. Soft light radiated from it, touching the bed as an invitation to climb back under the covers.

They left Lebanon in a buggy. After that they rode in the back of a farm wagon for twelve miles wedged between wooden boxes of freight. Deborah's resentment toward her father mounted the closer they came to the end of their journey. Each stop she hoped was the last, but another day and a half of hard travel passed before they pulled up on the north side of the square in the town of Stockton late Saturday afternoon.

"Reverend Smith?"

Deborah and her father both turned at the voice. Jacob nodded. "Yes, and you must be Aaron Stark's son. The resemblance is amazing."

Deborah looked into eyes bluer than she could have ever imagined. The fact that the man stood staring at her didn't at once occur to her as she stared back. This must be Dane Stark, the man she would be marrying. He was tall, a few years older than her, with unruly black hair curling in wild abandon on top of his head. His build was lean and muscular, his jaw strong, his features extremely handsome. But the haunted look in his sky-blue eyes drew her attention from the rest. Surely, this man had suffered greatly in recent days.

Without speaking to her, he turned and shook her father's hand. "I'm proud to meet you. I'm Dane Stark. My parents sent me to fetch you and your belongings to take to their house."

"Wonderful," Deborah's father said. "I look forward to seeing them again." He nodded toward Deborah. "This is my daughter, Deborah Renee, of whom we wrote."

As Dane's gaze fixed on hers again, Deborah felt a flush warm her face. He nodded and turned away. "I'll bring my wagon 'round and get your things loaded."

Deborah watched him cross the thick, green grass until he disappeared behind the courthouse, which sat on a patch of lawn in the center of the square.

Jacob stepped close to her side as he, too, watched Dane. "His mother says he is a dedicated Christian man, and like many in Cedar County, his sympathies lie with the preservation of our nation. I believe that is most admirable."

Deborah wondered why her father would try to convince her of Mr. Stark's attributes. Surely it made no difference to him whether she approved of her future husband. She hadn't approved of the first one, so why should this time be any different? A helpless feeling washed over her as she stood at the edge of the street watching the men load her heavy trunk into Mr. Stark's wagon.

Within minutes Deborah found a spot in the back of the wagon, leaving her father to sit in front with Dane as they rumbled west out of Stockton. She watched the gently rolling hills and longed for her mother and home. Even remaining under the strict dominion of her father for the rest of her life would be better than marrying a stranger and subjecting herself to an unknown future.

When the wagon turned north, Deborah turned her attention to the front seat where her father sat deep in conversation with Mr. Stark.

"Did you see much action during the war?"

Dane shook his head. "No major battles, thank God. We had our share of skirmishes, though. And with Kansas so close we were always on the lookout for Jayhawkers and bushwhackers alike."

"I understand your sympathies are with the North." Jacob looked at the younger man. "Does that hold true for the rest of your family?"

"All but one." Dane stared straight ahead. "Wesley, my brother just younger, has always had a mind of his own. Mother says he's the spittin' image of our uncle Ralph." His laugh held no mirth. "I'd reckon he's not the only one. I've got a cousin she says the same thing about."

"Ralph Stark," Jacob said. "Yes, I remember meeting him. Didn't your mother write about his passing several years back?"

"Probably." Dane nodded. "He died before the war started."

"This brother you mentioned," Jacob said, picking up the thread of their conversation. "Did he fight with the South?"

"Yep. He left to join the rebels more'n two years ago. We haven't heard from him but once in all that time. He still hasn't come home."

"I'm sorry to hear that. Your other brothers—what are they doing?"

"Ash and Levi fought together with the regulars. Joshua, too, just not with the twins. They've all been home several days now. Then I've got two baby brothers still at home."

Jacob nodded. "Where did you serve?"

"I served with the militia here in Stockton since the war started. Felt like I could do more good stayin' home defendin' my own land."

"That's quite admirable. A man must take care of what is rightfully his."

Deborah wondered at her father's eager acceptance of this young man. He seemed quite impressed with him. Just as he had been with Jamison, she recalled. Did he want to be rid of her so much that he would shove her off on anyone?

The two men talked of other things then. The countryside, crops, and the little church where they would be holding revival meetings. Deborah looked past Dane's broad shoulders to his strong jaw. From her vantage point behind and to the side of him, no one was paying attention to her, so she took time to study his profile.

His clean-shaven face revealed strong, regular features. She wished she could see his eyes. She knew they were blue, but she wanted to see past the color into his soul. Only then would she know if Dane Stark would be a good father to his children and a kind husband to her.

As Deborah listened to the men talk, the wagon rattled and jounced its way over the narrow dirt road to the Stark farm. They entered a plush meadow covered in thick, green, waist-high grass. Deborah sat straighter and looked about.

Dane followed the faint wheel tracks through the waving grass until it gave way to a log and frame house that looked as if it had grown from the meadow. Behind the house a small hill rose, leading the way into a large stand of trees.

The wagon jerked to a stop in front of the house. A woman who stood framed in the doorway stepped out into the sunshine. Deborah saw that although her step was light and quick, her light brown hair held highlights of gray. Laugh lines near the corners of her dark eyes and around her mouth added character to her still attractive face. Her smile included them all.

"Welcome to our home." She shook hands with Deborah's father as he stepped down from the wagon. "It's been a long time, hasn't it, Jacob, since we played as children on the streets of St. Louis?"

"That it has, Cora," Jacob agreed. "A long time, indeed."

"How is your sister Margaret? It's been more than a year since I've heard from her."

"She's well, but busy with her new grandson. I'm sure she'll write soon and tell you all about him."

Cora laughed. "So Margaret is a grandmother now? We are getting old, Jacob. I have two grandchildren myself." Her gaze shifted as Dane helped Deborah from the wagon. "This must be your daughter."

"Yes, Deborah Asberry." Jacob drew her forward. "Deborah, this is Mrs. Cora Stark, Dane's mother. I'm sure she will want to discuss the wedding arrangements with you later."

Deborah's heart sank. Surely this meant that Father approved of Dane. She looked into the woman's soft, brown-eyed gaze that seemed to envelop her in understanding and love. In spite of her natural reserve, Deborah smiled and offered her hand. "I'm pleased to meet you, ma'am."

Cora took Deborah's hand in hers and drew her close for a quick hug. "I'm so glad you agreed to come, Deborah. What you are doing means so much to us."

She stepped back and, still holding Deborah's hand, smiled. "Right now I need to get dinner on the table so we can eat. I imagine you're starved and worn out from the trip. In a day or two, after you've had a chance to look us over real good, we'll have us a talk. Just you and me."

Deborah hadn't expected to like anyone here, but she already knew she liked Mrs. Stark. She looked forward to the promised talk.

As she moved beside Mrs. Stark to the house, she glanced over her shoulder at Dane who had moved the wagon to the barn where he'd started unhitching the horses. He had ignored her for the most part. She wondered if he were also being forced into this marriage. No doubt, because of circumstances, he was.

❧

Deborah dried the last dish from their evening meal and placed it in the cupboard. Cora gave her a quick hug. "Thank you so much, Deborah. It's a real treat for me to have female help and company. What with a house full of boys, there's always been more dirtying than cleaning around here."

Deborah smiled. "I don't mind helping."

She glanced toward the front room of the house, wishing that the men would go outside. But the Starks' two younger sons were the only ones who hadn't stayed indoors. After they'd finished eating, Cora's husband suggested the men, all six of them, sit down and chew the fat while their dinner settled. Deborah assumed that meant talk since that's all they had been doing for the last half hour.

A quick rap at the door caught her attention. A pretty young woman stuck her head inside, a wide smile brightening her face. "Hi, is anyone home?"

"Lenore, come on in." Cora pulled the door open wider.

Deborah noticed Dane's eyes come alive when Lenore stepped into the room. She wondered at that until she saw the small bundle in Lenore's arms.

Dane stood and reached for the blanket-covered infant. "I sure do appreciate you keepin' an eye on my young'uns today."

Lenore smiled up at him. "It was my pleasure, I assure you."

Deborah watched as Dane took the baby and cradled it against his strong, muscular chest. He looked like he'd done the same thing many times, yet somehow his masculine presence dwarfed the tiny baby. Then a small boy burst through the open door and flung himself against Dane's legs.

"Daddy, I miss you whole bunch." He tilted his head back as far as he could to see his father's face.

Dane bent to scoop him up with his right arm while he held the sleeping baby in his left. Cora took a step forward. "Dane, be careful."

A fleeting grin broke the somber expression on his face for a moment. "Don't worry, Mom. I'm getting used to it."

The little boy's dark, curly hair, so like his father's, brushed Dane's neck as he snuggled close. His thumb found his mouth and his eyes closed in contentment.

Cora's eyebrows lifted. "How long has that been going on?" She nodded at the little boy sucking his thumb.

"Been doin' it off and on all day, I'd reckon." A young man

stepped through the still-open door and slipped his arm around Lenore.

Dane nodded toward the man. "Evenin', Billy. Thanks for bringin' Tommy and Beth over. I appreciate y'all keepin' 'em today."

"It was no trouble, Dane." Lenore spoke for her husband. "They are both little angels."

"Speakin' of angels, who's that you got hidin' in the kitchen?"

Deborah looked up to meet the bright blue eyes of the young man. A slow grin spread across his handsome face as his arm dropped from around his wife and he took a step toward her.

Cora moved forward, effectively stopping his progress. "Deborah, please excuse our manners. I'd like for you to meet Dane's cousin and his wife, Billy and Lenore Reid." She slipped her arm around Deborah's waist. "This is Deborah Asberry. She's come all the way from St. Louis to marry Dane and become a mother to his children."

Deborah watched shock register on Billy's and Lenore's faces as Mrs. Stark turned toward the men watching from the sitting room. "As you know, our church will be in revival this next week. Deborah's father, Reverend Jacob Smith, will be doing the preaching. I'll expect you two to be there every night."

Jacob stood and crossed the room to shake hands with the young couple. As he extended a second invitation for them to attend the revival meetings, Cora nudged Deborah.

"Why don't you go rest for a spell? I imagine you're worn-out after such a long journey."

Thankful for the older woman's understanding and kindness, Deborah slipped into the upstairs bedroom Cora pointed out and closed the door. Dane's cousins had obviously not been

told about her. Probably no one had been. She didn't suppose
an arranged marriage was something one would spread around
until they were sure of the outcome.

Deborah lay across the bed and closed her eyes. How she
wished she could go someplace far away where no one would
bother her. She almost laughed aloud at her foolishness.

For years their country had been ravaged by war. The
past few days, as Deborah and her father journeyed across
Missouri, they had seen evidence of destruction on every side
in the abandoned farms and burned-out hulls of once fine
homes. There was no place for a young woman alone to run.
Deborah knew without doubt that she must now depend on
a man whom she knew little about except that he didn't want
this marriage any more than she did.

three

Revival services began the following morning after Sunday school in the little one-room country church just a couple of miles from the Starks' house. The pastor, Brother Timothy Donovan, stepped back and gave Jacob freedom to conduct the services. Deborah sat beside Mrs. Stark on the second pew from the front and breathed a sigh of relief that she didn't have to sit with Dane since he had yet to arrive with his children.

She hadn't seen him since the day before when she hid from his cousin in the Starks' bedroom. After taking a much needed nap, she had returned to the other room to find that Billy and Lenore had gone home as had Dane and his children. She wasn't sorry to have missed them. If she never saw Dane or his cousins again, she wouldn't mind.

After the congregation sang several songs, Deborah stood and made her way to the front. She'd tried to get out of singing, but her father had been adamant. He insisted that God had given her a gift, and she would sin if she didn't use it for His glory. She gave in as she always did.

Deborah stood beside the pulpit with her hand resting on the edge. As the organist played the introduction, she scanned the congregation. There were few empty seats. She skimmed over the front rows until her gaze rested on the back pew where Dane sat alone with his two children. She assumed he had slipped in after the service started.

While she watched, his young son used Dane as a step-ladder so he could see out the open doorway behind them.

24

Something must have caught the little boy's attention. She tried to see and almost missed her cue. As she began to sing "Come Ye Sinners, Poor and Needy," she saw a large, brown dog scarcely ten feet from the door lift its shaggy head and smile inside at the little boy, its tongue hanging out one side of its mouth.

Then, as always happened when she sang, her mind and heart became lost in the beauty of the music and she forgot all else. She lifted her focus to a spot high on the back wall while she felt herself swept along on a rising crescendo of emotion that became her praise and worship to her Savior.

❧

Dane cradled his tiny baby daughter in one arm while he kept a firm grip on the shoulder strap of his small son's overalls. He'd missed Sunday school because Tommy kept getting into something and smearing it down the front of his shirt. After changing the little boy's clothing and washing his hands and face twice, he gave up on dressing the baby until he figured out how to keep Tommy clean.

Standing just inside the bedroom where he could peer around the doorframe at his son, he waited. Tommy, oblivious to his father, raced across the large room that served as both parlor and kitchen. Dane watched him climb on a chair he had pulled from the table to the pie safe and then he knew. The custard pie his mother had insisted he bring home the night before was the problem.

With long strides Dane raced across the floor and grabbed his son just as one chubby hand dipped into the destroyed pie.

Dane smiled now as he remembered Tommy's howl of frustration when he tried to insert his sweet-coated hand into his mouth and couldn't.

But now, as Deborah's song filled the church, Dane tightened his hold on Tommy and forgot all else but the beauty of her voice. Rich and vibrant, it caressed his soul, soothing the turmoil that had been his since Anne's death. When the song ended and she returned to her place beside his mother, he realized he had never heard a sweeter voice. Nor had he been touched so deeply by a song.

❧

After service that morning Deborah knew she would have to sing each evening of the revival as she accepted praise from one person after another. For as always happened, after the congregation heard her once, they would not let her rest until she sang again. Her father always said that Deborah's voice drew the crowds who must then listen to him preach.

She sighed as she made her way to the wagon past small clusters of men and women visiting. She dodged children running and playing, their childish voices calling out to one another as her mind returned to her problem. It wasn't that she didn't like to sing. She loved losing herself in the beauty of music and praise. But she had never been given a choice. For as long as she could remember, she had been told that she would sing. Just as now she had no choice in marriage.

As Deborah placed a toe on the wheel hub and grasped the rough wood of the wagon to hoist herself up, a hand closed around her arm.

"Here, let me help you." Dane's deep voice startled her so that she lost her balance and fell back against his chest.

"Oh, I'm so sorry." Her face flamed. She jerked away, turning to look up at him. He stood much too close.

His blue eyes crinkled at the corners as he smiled down at her. He was quite good-looking when he smiled. "It's my fault. I shouldn't have come up behind you like that without lettin' you know."

He looked from her to the big farm wagon. "I thought you might need some help gettin' up there."

"That's all right. I've climbed into wagons before all by myself." His presence brought a strange feeling in her chest. She didn't want his help. She looked away, glad to see his mother coming toward them with his baby in her arms.

"Dane, where are your manners? Aren't you going to help this girl into the wagon?" Cora smiled at them, and Deborah knew she would have to accept his assistance now.

Amusement lightened Dane's face as he looked down at Deborah. His eyebrows lifted and his bright blue eyes twinkled. "I was just gettin' to that, Mom, before you showed up."

Then, before Deborah could object further, he reached down to span her waist with his hands. As if she weighed nothing, he lifted her above his head and set her on the seat of the wagon.

Warmth that had nothing to do with the noonday sun beating down on her spread throughout Deborah's body. She had expected a helping hand. She certainly hadn't expected to feel like a sack of potatoes—or maybe like a young lady who had caught the eye of the most appealing man she had ever seen. She glanced at Cora and saw the smile of approval on her face. Sure that her cheeks were a brilliant red, Deborah stared at her hands that were clenched into balls in her lap. Unable to resist longer than a few seconds, she lifted her gaze to meet Dane's blue eyes, now cool with the spark of humor gone. Then Cora stepped between them.

"Deborah, would you mind holding the baby while I climb on board?"

Deborah looked at the tiny scrap of humanity that Cora lifted toward her. The encounter with Dane all but forgotten, she reached down, placing one hand under the baby's neck and shoulders, the other cradling her backside. She could not tear her eyes from the miniature face that slept so peacefully. Soft fuzz of blond—almost white—hair peeked out from around the pristine white bonnet that framed the baby's perfect features.

Deborah barely noticed scooting over to make room for Cora as she brought the infant close and cuddled her in her arms. She watched the tiny rosebud lips purse and suckle for a moment as if seeking comfort from the disruptions in her short life. A wave of pity broke over Deborah's heart, and she gently tightened her hold as if to assure the tiny child that all would be well.

Although she heard Dane and Cora talking, Deborah didn't listen, for at that moment a tiny, perfectly formed hand came free of the white lacy blanket and jerked in the air. Deborah placed her forefinger against the tips of the baby's fingers. Each finger couldn't have been bigger around than the crochet hook that had been used to make the blanket, yet when she gently pried them open they closed around her finger with surprising strength.

"She's a beautiful child, isn't she?" Deborah looked up at Cora's softly spoken words.

"I've never been around babies much."

"Why don't you hold her on the way home?" Cora suggested as her younger sons came running to the wagon, followed at a slower pace by Deborah's father and Aaron Stark.

The men climbed into the back while one of the boys squeezed in beside Deborah. He slapped the reins over the horse's back and they were off. As they pulled away, Deborah watched Dane scoop his small son up and head toward his own wagon.

Deborah held her precious charge close, reveling in the little, warm body that fit so well in the crook of her arm. A wave of maternal love surprised and frightened her as the baby's eyes opened and stared up at her in solemn scrutiny.

When they reached the Starks' house, she placed the baby

on a downstairs bed and joined Cora in the kitchen to help with dinner preparations. Deborah was thankful that the men remained outdoors until Cora called them in to eat.

After a dinner lightened by laughter and conversation, Deborah helped Cora clean up the well-picked-over table. Several minutes later, she hung the damp tea towel on a nail and followed Cora from the kitchen.

Dane now held his infant daughter. His eyes, cold and brooding, seemed to follow Deborah's every movement. Not knowing what else to do, Deborah stood behind her father's chair, wishing she would wake and find that the last several weeks were a horrible nightmare.

She listened to the men talk, although their conversation meant little to her. She imagined she felt Dane's gaze on her, but she refused to look.

"Daddy, go see kitties?" Tommy's childish voice stood out from the lower rumble of the adult voices.

Deborah glanced toward Dane. His son tugged on his sleeve. As she watched, Dane looked up and met her gaze. He handed the baby to his mother.

"All right, Tommy. Maybe we should show Mrs. Asberry the kitties, too. Why don't you go ask her?"

When the toddler turned his confident grin on her, Deborah wondered if he knew who she was. He ran across the room, stopped in front of her, and craned his neck to look into her face. One chubby little hand reached out and took her fingers.

"Wanna see my kitties, Miss 'Berry? Wiff me and mine daddy. Kitties in barn."

Deborah looked down at the little boy who continued to hold her hand and tug as if he would take her to his father. She shook her head. "No, thank you. Maybe another time."

As she tried to free her hand, her father turned in his chair and frowned at her. "Nonsense, Deborah. Run along with the boy and enjoy yourself. This will be a good opportunity for you young people to become better acquainted."

Deborah clenched her free hand, buried in the folds of her wide skirt, into a fist. She should have known better than to think she had a choice on even such a trivial matter. Without a word, she followed the little boy to the door, grabbing her bonnet as she went.

Deborah preceded Dane and Tommy into the bright sunshine. A strained silence hung between them as they walked across the yard until Deborah's steps lagged behind as much as Tommy's ran ahead.

"C'mon," Tommy called back to the adults. He waited at the barn door, bouncing first on one foot and then the other. "See kitties."

"We're comin'. Just hold your horses," Dane called to him before looking back at Deborah. "You makin' it okay?"

"Yes, I'm fine." She quickened her pace, even as her teeth gritted in frustration. As she hurried toward the barn, she breathed a prayer of petition. *Dear Lord, please help me accept my lot in life as is in keeping with Your will.*

Dane opened the heavy log door and Tommy ran inside. Dane stepped back and waited as Deborah brushed past before following her into the dim barn.

Specks of dust danced in long slanting rays of sunlight that entered through cracks in the walls. The musty scent of hay and animals created a strange combination to Deborah's city-bred senses. The huge barn felt cooler than outdoors and much more frightening. She glanced into the shadowy recesses of the stalls and wondered what might be hidden from view behind the walls. Then a rustle in the straw startled her, and she jumped with a tiny squeal.

"Don't worry. It won't hurt you. It's probably a rat or maybe just a tiny mouse." Dane stood several feet away. "That's what the kittens are good for. At least they will be when they get big."

At the first mention of rodents, a shiver chased down Deborah's spine. She instinctively stepped closer to Dane, her only thought to get away from the danger she couldn't see.

He grinned. "Honest, they won't bother you. They're just after the grain we put out for the horses."

When she cast him a disbelieving look, he laughed. "Come on. There's one place in this barn you can be sure there are no mice. Meow-meow won't let one within sight before she's got it caught."

"Meow-meow?" Deborah looked up at him. He seemed to be serious.

When he laughed again, she decided she enjoyed the sound. She supposed that was because he so seldom even smiled.

"My son named her. I reckon it fits since that's about the only thing she ever says." Dane looked down at her and grinned.

Deborah's heart froze. Did he have to be so handsome? Did he have to be so nice? Jamison wasn't as handsome, but he had been nice—until they were married. Then he had treated her as one might treat a child who didn't know her own mind. Dane would be the same. Deep in her heart she knew it, just as she knew there was not one thing she could do about it.

"You ready to see the kittens?" Dane took Deborah's arm, and she allowed him to lead her to the back of the barn where she could hear childish laughter. They found Tommy lying in a pile of straw with a kitten on his tummy, one batting at his hair, and another standing with its front paws against his side. A gray-and-white striped cat that Deborah assumed was Meow-meow lay nearby watching.

"Kitties like me, Daddy." Tommy grinned.

Dane squatted beside his son and picked up the one at his

side. He held the kitten out to Deborah. "Would you like to hold it?"

She took the tiny ball of gray fur and felt the vibration of its purr against her hand. As Dane turned back to his son and she watched father and son play, a feeling she didn't understand welled up within her heart. She couldn't remember her father ever playing with either her or her brother.

She thought of the sweet baby sleeping in the house and of the little boy who seemed ready to accept her presence. Maybe marriage to Mr. Stark wouldn't be so bad. The children needed a mother and she needed a home. For the first time since her father had told her she would be moving to southern Missouri to marry a widower with two children, she felt ready to accept her lot in life. She would marry Dane Stark and, with God's help, she would make a home for herself and be a mother to his two adorable children. Then, if God allowed, maybe soon she would have children of her own.

four

Monday morning Deborah descended the stairs from the tiny bedroom in which she had been sleeping. She crossed the living room and stopped outside the kitchen door. Cora sat at the table with her tiny granddaughter in her arms. Dane stood across from her holding his son.

Cora cuddled the baby as she smiled at Dane. "I'm going to miss this, but I believe you are doing the right thing. Deborah seems to be a wonderful girl."

"I reckon so." Dane didn't sound convinced. "I don't have a lot of choice in the matter."

"I guess not." Cora's smile never wavered. "But remember, son, good marriages have been made with less reason."

Deborah stepped back before either noticed her presence. As she stood in the middle of the floor wondering what she should do, Dane walked into the room. Surprise widened his eyes for a moment when he glanced her way. She tried to appear as if she had just come downstairs.

Expecting him to speak, she gave him a smile, getting a curt nod in response as he went outside.

She moved to the window and peeked out to see her father and Aaron Stark approach Dane. He seemed to have no trouble talking to them. Deborah didn't know whether she felt angry or amused at his actions. Mr. Dane Stark obviously didn't want to marry her any more than she wanted to marry him. What a plight they both were in!

"Miss 'Berry?" Deborah felt a tug on her skirt. She turned from the window as Tommy tugged her skirt again. "Me comed to see you."

Cora stood several feet away with the baby. A smile hovered around her lips. Deborah's face flamed. What must she be thinking? "I heard voices and. . ." Her voice trailed away.

Cora's smile spread. "Tommy and I thought you might be awake. Dane usually brings the little ones before the sun comes up. Farmers are notoriously early risers. It took me awhile to get used to crawling out of bed in the dark, but now I don't think I could sleep in if I tried."

Thankful that the older woman had graciously ignored her confusion, Deborah smiled. "I guess our city ways are quite different, but I'm sure I can adjust."

"You will do fine." Cora crossed into her bedroom just off the living room. "Baby Beth fell asleep in my arms. I'll put her on my bed, and then I'd better get breakfast on the table. If you heard the men outside, they will be underfoot before I'm ready for them."

"Miss 'Berry, I comed to see you," Tommy repeated with another tug on her skirt.

Deborah knelt beside the little boy and put her arm around him. At only two years of age, he seemed small to her, yet his shoulders felt sturdy under her touch. She smiled at him. "I'm glad you did. We'll have lots of fun today, won't we?"

"Yes." He nodded. "Daddy come get me."

"That's right." Deborah wondered if he worried that his daddy might leave as his mother had. Her heart softened toward this tiny replica of Dane Stark. No wonder Dane felt such a need to provide a mother for his children.

Cora was stirring the gravy when the men came in from outdoors. Deborah didn't think she would ever get used to the noise of so many men and boys as the Stark family boasted. Her father seemed to enjoy their constant talk and roughhousing. Deborah wondered at that since he insisted that she and her brother always behave with the utmost decorum at home as befitted the children of a minister of God.

Dane's five younger brothers ranged in age from twelve to twenty-five. Deborah had heard them talk about another brother a year younger than Dane. The black sheep of the family, as his brothers sometimes called him, Wesley left home at the beginning of the war to join the Confederate Army. As the first year rolled into another, he sent one letter, but not once had he made an appearance. Deborah could see the worry in Cora's and Aaron's eyes when anyone mentioned Wesley's name. Not one spoken prayer ended without a plea for his safe return.

Cora poured the gravy into a bowl and set it on the table then sat in the chair held for her by her youngest son, Benjamin. As soon as Benjamin sat down, Aaron bowed his head and asked the blessing on their breakfast.

After the men left, Deborah helped Cora clean while Tommy finished his breakfast. He then climbed from the table and announced that he was going outside.

Cora smiled at her grandson and turned to Deborah. "Would you like to keep an eye on him? There's a spring over by the woods that is beautiful this time of year. I made the mistake of taking Tommy there, and he's tried to go alone more than once."

"Are you sure you don't mind? I expected to help with the housework." Deborah looked out the open kitchen door into the sun-brightened yard beyond. What would her father think if she neglected the household duties to go outside and play?

"You've already helped more than enough. Besides, you will find that watching Tommy is no picnic. Don't worry about little Beth. I'll be right in the house where I can hear her when she wakes."

A flush moved through Deborah's body. She had forgotten the baby. What kind of mother would she be to forget a child in her care? She managed a weak smile and a murmur of agreement before following Tommy outdoors.

"See kitties," Tommy announced as his sturdy little legs carried him toward the barn.

Rats and mice lived in the barn. Deborah shuddered. She watched Tommy trudging ahead and realized he wouldn't turn back without a fuss. With a resigned sigh, she followed, catching up with the little boy at the barn door.

"Hey, Tommy, what are you doin' out here?" One of Dane's brothers stepped into the sunshine from the interior of the barn. He nodded toward Deborah with a quick grin.

"Unca Levi, me comed to see kitties." The little boy seemed to forget Deborah as he ran through the wide, open space in the middle of the barn and disappeared in its depths. Levi laughed.

"He sure likes those kittens."

Deborah smiled. Twins Levi and Ashton looked no more alike than any of the other brothers. Levi had light brown eyes like his mother. His hair wasn't as dark as Dane's, and he wasn't as good-looking.

Heat crept into her cheeks as soon as she realized where her thoughts had gone. She looked away toward the back of the barn where she could hear Tommy's laughter.

She gestured toward the sound. "I'd better keep an eye on him."

"Sure. See ya 'round." Levi moved on out the door and walked away, whistling as he went. He carried some sort of long-handled tool with a sharp blade that Deborah couldn't have named if she'd tried.

She turned back to the interior of the barn and cringed. Only one path led to Tommy, with furry scavengers lurking on either side. She took a deep breath and stepped forward.

"Tommy." Maybe the sound of her voice would send the rodents running in the opposite direction. She called again halfway through the barn. "Tommy."

A sound to her right sent her running the rest of the way with a sharp squeal. "Tommy!"

Tommy stood and looked up at Deborah with wide, blue eyes. "Want mine mommy."

Deborah didn't know how to answer. "Grandma's in the house."

Tommy stared at her a moment and then ran toward the front of the barn. She threw out her hands in frustration. She wouldn't have taken the chance of running into a mouse if she'd known she would have to run the gauntlet a second time so soon.

Leaving the safety of Meow-meow's presence, Deborah ran as fast as she could after Tommy. Again she called his name hoping to scare away any rodent brave enough to make an appearance.

Deborah burst through the doorway into the outdoors and breathed a sigh of relief until she wondered if Tommy might be deaf—she had called his name at least three times and he hadn't even slowed. Already he was halfway to the house. How could such a small person cover ground so quickly? She ran to catch up.

Tommy reached the house as Deborah reached Tommy. "Are you running away from me, Tommy?"

Without sparing her a glance, he jerked the front door open and ran through. "Gamma. Gamma, me want you."

"Slow down, Tommy." Cora stepped around the table as the little boy launched himself at her. "What's your hurry?"

"Want you."

Cora lifted her grandson and settled him on her hip. He

gave her a hug and then squirmed to get down. Deborah watched Cora laugh and set him on the floor. She wondered if this was normal behavior for a two-year-old. Since Cora didn't seem to be concerned, she assumed it was.

"So have you already tired of playing outside?" Tommy ran into the parlor ignoring his grandmother. Cora shook her head with an indulgent smile as he disappeared into the other room.

"I'm so sorry." Deborah felt as if she had failed her first attempt at making friends with her future stepson. What kind of mother would she be? She couldn't remember the baby, and she couldn't keep up with the little boy.

Cora gave her a puzzled look. "What do you have to be sorry for?"

"I was supposed to keep Tommy occupied outside." Deborah was glad her father hadn't seen her pitiful attempts at motherhood. He would have scolded her if he had, and she felt bad enough already.

"You've done nothing to be sorry about." Cora washed her hands and dried them on a towel hanging on the end of the table that held the washbasin. "Tommy doesn't stay anyplace long. You'll get used to him."

She pulled a large ball of bread dough from the mixing bowl on the table. Placing it on a pile of flour on a cloth-covered board, she began kneading.

Deborah wasn't sure she wanted to get used to Tommy, or Beth either, for that matter. She knew nothing about small children and babies. She stepped near the door leading into the living room and watched Tommy play with a horse carved from wood with deep red streaks running through it. The craftsmanship intrigued her. The horse looked so real as Tommy made it gallop across the floor.

She had noticed the chairs in the kitchen, too, had intricate designs carved in the backs. Eight chairs sat around the Starks' long table and each had a different variety of flower that seemed to have been taken from its natural surroundings and placed on each chair by a master carver. When she had commented on them, Cora said Aaron had carved them. Such works of beauty would have brought top price in St. Louis.

"Go outside."

Deborah looked down into Tommy's upturned face. She smiled at the little boy. "Okay, let's go out and play."

For the rest of the morning, Deborah spent her time running after Dane's young son. By noon she realized Mrs. Stark was right. Watching young Thomas Wayne Stark and keeping him out of trouble was no picnic. Spring housecleaning, even with her mother's high standards, had been an easier job.

She helped Tommy wash his hands at the washbasin and then got him settled into a chair at the table. Cora gave her a smile as she passed by with a steaming bowl of corn. "Thanks, Deborah. You've done so much already this morning, I hate to ask, but I hear little Beth crying. Would you mind getting her?"

"Of course not." Deborah noticed her father's nod of approval as she gladly left the noisy confusion of the male-dominated kitchen for the relative quiet of Cora's bedroom. As she opened the door, the baby's cries became louder. How had Mrs. Stark heard her over the scraping chairs and voices of her sons when Deborah had heard nothing until the baby's crying was brought to her attention?

She felt a measure of satisfaction for her morning's work. She had chased Tommy all over the meadow, visited the kittens in the barn three times, popped back into the house twice—mostly she suspected so Tommy could reassure himself that his grandmother was still there—and even managed to play some games with the little boy. She didn't know how Tommy felt about her, but she suspected she could easily lose her heart to the adorable toddler.

Beth was another matter, however. At barely two months of age, she was so tiny and helpless. Deborah closed the bedroom door and crossed the room to sit on the bed beside the baby. She had held her once on the ride home from church and felt she could love her as if she were her own baby if only she knew what to do with her.

Right now for instance. One touch told Deborah that she was about to learn how to change a diaper. If she didn't do it right away, Mrs. Stark would be coming to see why the baby still cried.

"Shh, little Beth. It's all right. Let's not cry now." Deborah gingerly slid one hand under the infant's soggy diaper and another under her back and neck, lifting until she held her against her chest. She patted the tiny back, pleased that the crying had stopped. Now to find a clean diaper and figure out what to do with it.

Finding a stack of folded diapers on the corner of the dresser wasn't hard. Mrs. Stark probably kept a supply on hand since she had been watching the children for Dane. With one hand supporting the baby, Deborah took a diaper from the stack. She turned and lowered Beth to the bed.

"Everything all right in here?" Mrs. Stark slipped in the door.

"Oh." Deborah looked up with a tremulous smile. "I was just going to try changing her diaper. She's pretty wet."

Cora laughed. "That doesn't surprise me. Do you need help?"

"I've never changed a diaper before. I don't know if I know how."

"Not a thing to it." Cora brushed her concerns aside as she sat on the opposite side of the bed. "If this one's just wet, it'll be perfect to practice on."

Deborah's heart sank. She hadn't thought that the diaper

might be more than just wet. Her concerns must have shown on her face, because Cora laughed again.

"You'll get the hang of it all soon enough."

Cora talked Deborah through the simple steps of changing the diaper. When she finished, Deborah picked Beth up and held her close in her arms. Beth watched her with bright blue eyes, bringing a smile to Deborah's lips and chastisement to her heart. How could she have forgotten such a precious baby this morning?

"I want you to know how much all of us appreciate your willingness to marry Dane and become a mother to his children." Cora patted Deborah's arm. "It can't be easy. Leaving everything you know to come to a backwoods place like this. I know how it was for me, and I had my entire family around me. I missed St. Louis so much back then. Little did I know this place would become more home to me than St. Louis ever was. I hope you feel the same way in time. If it's all right with you, we can have the ceremony on Sunday before your father returns to St. Louis."

Deborah didn't know what to say. Cora surely didn't know that she had no choice—that if she went against her father's wishes she might very well have no home to go back to. She simply nodded her agreement and was almost glad when the baby began fussing.

"She's probably hungry. I have a bottle fixed for her in the kitchen." Cora stood. "Would you like to feed her?"

"If you don't mind."

"Not at all. There's a rocking chair in the living room. I imagine you are ready for a rest after chasing after Tommy all morning." Cora smiled before going out the door. "He takes a long nap in the afternoon."

By the time Dane returned for his children, Deborah was ready for a good night's sleep. Not that his children were especially hard to care for. They were just so busy when they weren't sleeping. During Tommy's nap, Beth stayed awake. Deborah soon learned that tiny babies demand attention every bit as much as toddlers do.

Dane stayed for supper, sitting at the table across from Deborah, yet ignoring her as if she didn't exist. She wished she could do the same. Although she managed to keep her gaze averted, she could think of little else. She was glad when they finished eating and Dane left with his children.

That evening at church, as Deborah went forward to sing, her gaze moved to the back where Dane sat with his little ones. Then, as she allowed her heart and soul to lift in praise to the Savior, she forgot about Dane, his children, her father, and everything except for the words she sang and the beauty of the music.

➴

Two more days slipped by without Dane making a move to speak to Deborah about the wedding. Not that Deborah minded. The less she had to do with him, the better she liked it. But she knew he would not ignore her forever, especially after they were married. On Thursday evening after church, Dane asked if he could escort her home, and she turned to her father for permission.

"Yes, that's a fine idea. This young man can serve as your chaperone." He placed his hand on Tommy's head and smiled down at him.

Deborah had expected her father to accompany them. To assign the duties of chaperone to a two-year-old showed how little he cared for her. She turned away to meet Cora's smile.

"It will be fine, Deborah. Dane is honorable, and Tommy is probably a better chaperone than most adults would be. Go on and see if you can't get my son to talk to you. You need to become better acquainted."

Dane helped Deborah climb onto the wagon seat before lifting Tommy to sit beside her. Deborah scooted over so that Dane would have room to sit beside his son.

"I thought you might like to see my place first before it's too dark." Dane spoke as they started off. "We'll drive by."

"Yes, I would like that." Deborah hadn't thought about the house she would be living in. She had resigned herself to this marriage with little more enthusiasm than one might give a life sentence.

"Mine house." Tommy nodded.

"Yeah, we're going to show the pretty lady your house."

Deborah caught her breath. Dane didn't say more, and she wondered if he had intended to call her pretty. Probably not. Tommy chattered endlessly about his house, the horses, and everything they saw between the church and the house. Deborah understood why Cora thought Tommy would make a good chaperone. If they had tried, they couldn't have gotten a word in edgewise.

Dane pulled into the yard and stopped in front of the house. "We won't go inside, but this is home. My mother lived here with her parents when they first came to the country."

Deborah looked at the log cabin and smiled. It had a homey appearance to it as if just waiting for a family to move in.

"My uncle Ben and aunt Esther lived here after my grandmother died and my grandfather moved to Springfield. Uncle Ben is a missionary to the Indians in the West now. My mother's youngest brother lived here for a few years before he and his wife joined Uncle Ben on the missionary field. The house set empty after that until I moved in four years ago."

When Dane fell silent, Deborah wondered if she should say something. But what? *I'm looking forward to living here with you?* That would not be the truth.

Then he spoke again, rescuing her. "I have no idea why

you agreed to marry me and take on these kids. I know your husband recently died and I'm sorry for that. I think you need to know that I will never love you as a husband should love his wife."

Deborah looked over Tommy's head into Dane's serious gaze. What did he mean by that? She shook her head. "I don't understand why you are telling me this."

Dane looked away and Tommy remained silent. "My wife died when Beth was born. I will never again put another woman in that danger."

"Are you saying—"

"Yes." He looked back at her. "That's exactly what I'm saying. This is where we will live as husband and wife in name only. We will live together in this house, but we will not share a bed. If that isn't all right with you, now's the time to speak up."

five

Deborah sat in stunned silence, staring at Dane. She had never thought much about children until this past week. Caring for Dane's two little ones had brought out a maternal side to her that she hadn't known existed. She knew that if Jamison had lived, they would likely have had children. But now she would never have any. Must she be content to raise someone else's children?

"Do you have any objections?" Dane broke into her thoughts.

She focused on his face then looked away. "My father says I must marry you as it is my Christian duty to help a brother in need. I have never gone contrary to my father's demands and will not now. You seem to be a reasonable man, and I already adore your children. If you wish a marriage of convenience, I have no objections."

Then why did she feel as if he had rejected her? And why did it hurt so much? She should be glad that he would leave her alone. She had found Jamison's attentions undesirable; why would Dane's be any different? She stole a glance at him and saw the set line of his jaw.

"Fine. I'll get you back to my folks' then." He flicked the reins, and the wagon moved out.

They rode in silence for several minutes before Dane spoke. "There is one thing. I'd appreciate you keeping this between the two of us. It's no one else's business."

What did he think she would do? Tell everyone she met that her husband's only interest in her was as housekeeper and mother to his children? She noticed that Tommy had fallen asleep against his father's leg. No wonder he'd been so quiet.

"I assure you that I will tell no one. Furthermore, I will do my best to keep all appearances as if we have a normal relationship." She thought of her father and would have smiled if she hadn't been so hurt by Dane's rejection. Father would be surprised if he knew why Dane had asked to take her on this drive.

"Thank you." Dane stopped the wagon in front of his parents' house. He scooped Tommy up and twisted on the seat. A wooden box behind the seat held straw covered by a blanket. He lowered the little boy to the makeshift bed and met Deborah's curious gaze. "I can't drive the wagon and hold two babies. Beth is safe in the box, and Tommy does pretty well up here with me when he's awake."

"I see." Deborah's heart softened toward this young father who tried to be everything to his two motherless babies. She thought of her prayer the day Jamison was buried. She had asked God to help her submit to her father's rule even before she knew of Dane and his children. How could she let pride stand between her and the work God had set before her? She turned to climb down from the wagon.

"Just a minute." Dane stopped her. "I haven't officially asked you to marry me, and I'd like to do that. Now that you understand how I feel about things, will you, Deborah Asberry, agree to be my wife in name only?"

Deborah glanced down at the little boy sleeping behind them and back at Dane's steady gaze. "Yes, I will."

"I think they are planning the wedding for Sunday after church. Is that all right with you?"

Her smile held a touch of bitterness. *As if either of us has much choice.* She nodded. "That will be fine."

"Did Mom tell you about the party Saturday night after service? I imagine she invited the entire community."

Deborah nodded. "Yes, she mentioned it."

"Can you. . ." He looked away, then back to search her face. "Can you act like you're happy about all of this and stand beside me to greet our neighbors? I've known these people all my life."

Deborah understood that he thought she might embarrass him in front of his friends and family. He wanted everyone to think they would have a normal marriage. She wanted the same thing, didn't she? Then why did she feel so empty when she thought of living in Dane Stark's house day after day, always knowing that he didn't care for her?

"I'll do the best I can."

He smiled his approval, and Deborah lowered her gaze. Dane was the best-looking man she had ever met. She had recognized that at their first meeting, but she had assumed he would be like Jamison—overbearing and even cruel at times. Maybe that would come later after he became accustomed to her presence. She could only hope not.

He jumped from the wagon and came around to her side. As he helped her climb down, she looked back and asked, "Will Tommy be all right out here?"

"I'll just walk you to the door and get Beth. He'll be fine no longer than that."

At the door he stopped before opening it and looked down at her. "Thank you."

Deborah knew that Dane felt gratitude for her sacrifice. For surely their marriage would be a sacrifice to her. In less than three days she would be bound to a man who cared nothing for her and refused to give her children of her own. She would be forever giving up the chance for a real marriage with a man who loved her. But was there such a man, anyway? Jamison had never loved her although he had used her, just as Dane intended to do in a different way. Why, then, did

Dane's rejection hurt so much, while she had felt nothing but repulsion for Jamison's attentions?

❧

On Saturday evening, Deborah dressed with care. During the week of the revival meetings she had met most of the people who would converge on the Starks' cabin to express their congratulations and best wishes to Dane. She knew that he wanted his friends to accept her. She hoped to make the best possible impression on both Dane and his friends and family.

At the close of the service, Deborah again found herself riding to the Starks' with Dane and Tommy. Beth lay cuddled close in Deborah's arms. Dane drove past the house to stop the wagon out by the barn. "I hope you don't mind the walk," he said as if he had just realized she was with him. "The yard will be full, and I wanted to leave room for the others near the house."

"No, this is fine." She smiled down at the baby in her arms. Already the tiny girl had captured her heart. Tommy, too. Even if she could back out of this marriage now, she wouldn't. At first she had thought her father asked too much of her. Now, as she allowed her love to reach out to the two small children, she knew that God was giving her so much more in return.

Deborah waited while Dane took care of the horses and then together they walked to the house. Dane carried Tommy while Deborah carried Beth. Already she felt a part of his family, although she knew that position would never really be hers.

A festive atmosphere had overtaken the cabin. As Dane had predicted, wagons filled the yard and barn lot. The Starks' roomy cabin became crowded within minutes. Dane held the door for Deborah as she entered the parlor.

"Here're the lovebirds now." Billy Reid's voice carried over the others.

Deborah would have liked to hide her burning face when

half the gathering turned to stare at her and Dane. Then Cora moved forward with a warm smile. She stepped between Deborah and most of the guests as she reached for her granddaughter.

In a low voice, she said, "Don't mind Billy. He likes to stir things up, but he doesn't mean anything by it."

Cora held the baby against her shoulder and patted her back. "Why don't you two move around the room and visit with your guests? I'll watch Beth and Tommy."

At that moment, Cora's husband joined them. "Hey, how's my favorite grandson?"

Tommy lunged for his grandfather and the two went off together. Cora laughed. "I guess that takes care of that. Now go on, both of you. And don't let Billy bother you."

"Thanks, Mom." Dane took Deborah's arm and spoke close to her ear. "If Billy gets out of line, I'll take care of him."

They moved through the room, speaking to each guest. Deborah could place a few names with faces but didn't remember everyone. The pastor of the church, Timothy Donovan, and his wife, Grace, were there. Deborah recognized several members of the large Newkirk family. Dane introduced her to the Seymours, the Sinclairs, the Jordans, and so many more that she couldn't keep track.

Everyone seemed to welcome her with smiles and best wishes as if she and Dane had made a love match. If they knew, how would they act then? Deborah wondered.

A woman stepped to Deborah's side and gave her a warm hug. "Hi. I've never been in the right place at the right time to meet you, Deborah, but I enjoyed your singing in the revival. You have a beautiful voice. How wonderful that you are using your talent for the Lord."

"Thank you." Deborah looked into bright blue eyes. The woman's hair, as black as a moonless night, shimmered with highlights of gray, which added to her beauty.

Dane stood close to Deborah. "This is my aunt Ivy, my father's sister. She is Billy Reid's mother."

"I'm pleased to meet you." Deborah smiled at the older woman, realizing now that she must be close to fifty although she looked much younger.

Ivy smiled. "I'm glad to meet you, too, Deborah. I will be praying for both of you that as the years pass, your marriage will grow to be as filled with love and mutual understanding as mine was."

"Thank you, Aunt Ivy."

Deborah remained silent.

The older woman patted Deborah's arm and laughed softly. "There was a time when I did not serve the Lord. I made life miserable for everyone around me, but all I wanted was love and acceptance. I thought I'd found that when I married Bill and he took me to that big, fancy house of his." She laughed again. "The house soon became common, and I found that my husband didn't always understand me." She paused. "It wasn't until I turned my life over to Jesus Christ and accepted His forgiveness that I found the love I really needed. From that point on, I had the best life possible."

A faint smile crossed Deborah's lips. "I have already learned that Jesus's love is all I need, Mrs. Reid."

Deborah sensed Dane stiffen beside her. She didn't look at him, but she knew he understood that she meant she didn't need his love.

Ivy laughed and touched Dane's arm while she kept her other hand on Deborah's arm. "That is true, Deborah, but don't turn from the extra crumbs that the Master may throw under His table. Bill and I did not marry for love, either, yet we loved each other very much." She looked from one to the other. "I will be praying for you both that this marriage of convenience turns into a marriage of love."

With that, Ivy released them and turned away. Deborah watched her walk across the room to visit with another woman as if she had not just opened a wound that could not be healed.

Dane cleared his throat. "My aunt is outspoken. Like Billy, only in a nicer way."

Deborah looked up at him and saw his half smile of apology. She shrugged. "That's all right. I'm sure she doesn't understand the situation."

"Deborah. Dane. There you are." Cora motioned for them to join her.

Cakes and pies had been brought in for the reception. The ladies cut and handed out pieces until they were gone. Then someone cleaned off the table and piled gifts on it for the bride and groom. Again they were called forward to acknowledge the thoughtfulness of everyone there. They received hand-sewn linens, embroidered pillowcases, dresser scarves, and a tablecloth. A Single Wedding Ring quilt came from Billy and Lenore Reid.

Deborah wondered at the lavish gift. Surely Lenore had made this quilt for another purpose and decided to give it to her husband's cousin when she had nothing else ready.

She smiled at Lenore. "Thank you for such a lovely gift. I'm sure we will treasure it always."

Lenore lifted her eyebrows with a half smile. "You are quite welcome. I wanted to give something you could both use."

Deborah knew that all of the gifts had been gathered from the meager possessions of people who had gone through four years of war with both outlaws and soldiers taking whatever caught their eye. She appreciated the generosity of Dane's family and neighbors and, as she had said, would treasure each gift. Most had given from their hearts. She wondered about Lenore. Something didn't seem right. Almost as if she knew their marriage would not be real.

Dane waited until everyone else had gone; then he asked Deborah to step outside where they could speak privately. She walked a short distance from the house with him.

"I want to thank you for what you did tonight."

She looked up at him in confusion. "I didn't do anything."

His smile seemed sad. "Yeah, you did. You acted like everything was okay even when Lenore and Billy said things. They can be a trial, but you didn't let them ruffle your feathers."

Dane's approval meant more to Deborah than she wanted to admit. She smiled at him. "They didn't bother me too much."

He gave her a nod and walked her back to the house. Just when he seemed to be warming up to her, he grew cold again. She sighed. If they couldn't truly be husband and wife, couldn't they at least be friends? After all, they would be living in the same house, working together, and making a home for his children. It would seem the Lord had more work for her to do than first met the eye.

A few minutes later, as Deborah prepared for bed, her father knocked on her door. "Deborah, may I speak to you?"

She slipped into her robe and opened the door. "Come in, Father."

Deborah sat on the edge of the bed and was surprised when her father sat beside her and took her hands in his. "Tomorrow you will be married."

"For the second time, Father." She couldn't help reminding him and wished she had enough courage to mention the fact that both were his choice.

"Yes." He nodded. "You have been blessed to find two such wonderful Christian men. May God's blessing be on this union that you may have a long, happy marriage, fruitful in the work of the Lord."

Deborah almost choked at her father's words. She wondered what he would say if he knew that her second marriage would not be the fruitful union he thought. Would he call it off? Did she even want him to? She thought of Beth and Tommy and knew that she didn't. She wanted to be their mother. She could live with Dane as friends if she could get past the wall he had erected between them. This was the work God had given her to do—to banish the sorrow from Dane's eyes and to mother his children. Not an easy task, she knew, but one that she could do with God's help.

"I'll be leaving early Monday morning, and before I go, I want you to know that I'm proud of you, Deborah. God will bless you as you work for Him."

Deborah looked at her father while conflicting emotions of love and anger warred in her heart. Could she ever find the grace she needed to forgive her father for taking her so far from her mother and brother and for forcing her into two loveless marriages?

six

Deborah awoke on Sunday morning to the noise of Dane's two youngest brothers scuffling in the next room. The scent of frying bacon drifted up the stairs into her room, causing her stomach to turn. She threw the covers back. No doubt hunger stirred her stomach, but she knew that some of the turmoil she felt came from anxiety over the coming ceremony—and afterward.

Today was her wedding day. Never had she missed her mother more! She swung her feet to the floor and sat up, putting self-pity away. She had learned long ago that feeling sorry for herself never helped. The wedding would go on no matter how she felt. Her father would see to that. She might as well make the best of things.

She looked around the tiny bedroom, its sloped ceiling making it seem more of a hideout than an actual room. Her wedding dress hung on the wall beside the door. The dress she had worn when she and Jamison were married was safely stored at her parents' house. Her mother had helped her choose this dress as one they both believed would be appropriate for a second wedding. Cut in simple lines, lace covered the cream-colored silk underbodice. The full skirt attached to the bodice just below her natural waistline emphasized her slender figure. She would put on her wedding dress at the church after services.

&

Dane stood back and watched Deborah. She had dutifully stayed by his side throughout most of the meal but was now standing alone on the edge of the crowd. For the first time he thought beyond the needs of his children to what this marriage might mean to Deborah. Who was he to force her this way? To make her marry him when she'd rather head back home with her father in the morning. Why would she want to tie herself to him when he couldn't even offer her a real marriage?

Of course he had given her a chance to back out when he asked her to marry him Thursday night. She'd said yes. He could tell that she liked his little ones. Her father seemed to think the marriage was a good idea. Maybe Deborah wanted this. She'd been married before. Maybe she'd loved her husband so much she figured she'd never fall in love again.

"Why ain't ya over there with her instead of standin' here lookin'? Shame to see a pretty girl like that go to waste gettin' married to you."

"Well, if it isn't Billy Reid." Dane turned toward his cousin. "Seems I could say the same about you and Lenore. Where's your wife?"

Billy raised one dark eyebrow. "What's it to you?"

"Nothing." Dane sighed. "I was just making polite conversation."

"Yeah? Seems to me you always were too interested in Lenore."

"Where would you get an idea like that? I had a wife I loved very much."

"Yeah, and now you're about to get another one that you don't care a fig about."

Dane stared at his cousin. "Whether I do or don't care about my wife is none of your concern."

"Jist see that you don't care too much about mine."

Billy spoke low, but Dane heard as he walked away. He had never cared for Lenore the way Billy seemed to think, but he wasn't so sure about his feelings toward Deborah. His wife? Deborah would never be his wife for real. Why should that make him feel as if he were missing something just outside his grasp? A marriage in name only was what he wanted, wasn't it?

He stopped beside Deborah. "Hi. Are you all right?"

She smiled at him. "Of course. A little nervous, maybe, but otherwise I'm fine."

He cleared his throat. "Are you sure you want to go through with this?"

When she looked at him as if she didn't understand, he said, "The wedding. Marrying me. Being a mother to my kids."

"I already love Beth and Tommy. I just hope they can care for me a little."

"I doubt there's any problem with that."

She laughed. "I don't know. I've never been around children before. I have no idea how to care for them."

He grinned. "Most parents don't when they first start."

"I suppose not."

"Dane. Deborah. There you are." Deborah's father joined them, a wide smile on his face. "Dane, if you will go into the church, we'll be along shortly."

Dane noticed that most of the people were already heading toward the church door and realized that if Deborah was going to back out it had better be now. He caught her gaze and asked, "Are you sure?"

She nodded, giving him a sweet smile. "Yes, I'm sure. Go on."

Dane gave a quick nod and turned toward the church. Inside, he headed for the front and stood to one side. Deborah had requested that they have no attendants, so Dane stood alone with Pastor Donovan in front of a full church and watched the back door. The organist began playing a song he scarcely listened to. He wiped his hands on his trousers, and then Deborah and her father stepped through the open doorway. Dane watched his bride walk with her back straight, her head held high. Each step she took seemed to declare her determination to get through the ordeal before her with as much dignity as possible. His heart hurt for her.

Dane stepped forward to accept Deborah's hand from her father, then turned to face the minister. He promised himself at that moment that even though their marriage could never be real, he would see that Deborah's life with him was as pleasant as he could make it.

"Dearly beloved, we are gathered together. . . ." The traditional ceremony continued to the end as they promised to care for each other in sickness and in health. "I now pronounce you husband and wife."

Pastor Donovan looked at Dane. "You may now kiss the bride."

Dane stared at the older man he had known all his life as the words penetrated his brain. Kiss Deborah? How could he have forgotten this part of the ceremony? He turned to his bride. She looked frightened. He couldn't very well announce to the waiting congregation that he didn't want to kiss his wife, could he?

He gave her what he hoped was a reassuring smile and took her into his arms. She felt so tiny—and soft—and warm. Her hands touched his chest. As he leaned closer, they slid up to circle his neck. His lips touched hers, and he became lost in the sweetest kiss of his life. Emotions threatened to choke him when he finally pulled away. He couldn't care for Deborah. Not after only one week of barely seeing or talking to her. How could this be?

He stepped back and her hands slid away. He couldn't think right now, but soon after they were at home, he would sort out these feelings and figure out what to do. Somehow he had to keep his distance from Deborah. He could not break the vow he'd made the night Anne died. He could not place a second wife in danger of death just because of his own unbridled emotions.

He took a slow breath to quiet his racing heart and faced the congregation with Deborah by his side as Pastor Donovan said, "May I present to you, Mr. and Mrs. Dane Stark."

❧

Deborah stood beside the wagon and gave her father a parting hug. "You've made me proud today, Deborah. Mrs. Stark says someone goes into Stockton occasionally where letters can be mailed, so you be sure to write and let us know how you are doing. I'll tell your mother about the wedding as I know she will want the details."

"Please tell Mother and Caleb both that I love them and I will write as soon as I can." Deborah still felt anger toward her father. He seemed happy to leave her here among strangers. How did she know Dane would not be cruel to her? All that mattered was getting rid of her. Well, he had done that so now he could leave, and if she never saw him again she wouldn't care. Yet, deep in her heart she knew she did care and that made the pain so much harder to bear.

Dane appeared by her side and shook hands with her father. "Thank you, sir."

Deborah stepped back as they talked. She swiped at the moisture in her eyes and crossed the yard to Cora and the children. Cora gave her a warm hug while she held Beth in her other arm. "Are you all right?"

Deborah nodded. "I'm fine. I was just telling my father good-bye. May I hold the baby?"

As Cora handed Beth to her, Deborah knew that she needed the warmth and love that only a baby snuggled in her arms could give. She held little Beth close and marveled that she fit so perfectly with her head resting in the hollow of her shoulder. Deborah could feel tiny puffs of breath on her neck.

She rested her cheek against the downy softness of the baby's hair and patted her back, taking in the sweet smell of powder and baby.

"You look natural holding her," Cora said.

Deborah smiled. "I must confess, I didn't expect to feel natural, but I think I'm getting the hang of holding her, at least."

"Are you ready to go?" Dane asked.

She turned to look at him, unsure if he meant her. But of course he did. They were married now whether she felt like his wife or not. Whether she would ever feel like his wife. She nodded. "Yes. Any time you are."

Tommy grabbed Dane's leg. "Me go, too."

Dane scooped him up and set him on his shoulders to Tommy's delight. "I guess that's everyone, then."

"Deborah—" Cora lay a detaining hand on Dane's arm. "Just a minute. I had the leftovers from the dinner put in the back of your wagon. There should be enough for several meals. Most of it should keep a day or two, but you can put any perishables in the cellar. Just be sure to wrap it good."

Deborah didn't know the condition of Dane's kitchen. He had been taking his evening meals at the older Starks' each day this past week. Could it be that he had no foodstuff for her to cook? Is that why the women had fixed enough to last a few days? As she thanked his mother, she wondered what she might be walking into. She hadn't even seen the inside of the house.

Twenty minutes later she stepped into Dane's house and tripped over a boot that had fallen beside the door.

"Are you all right?" Dane steadied her, then just as quickly pulled his hand away and stepped back.

"Yes, I'm fine."

She no sooner spoke than Dane picked up his boots and

threw them up the stairs that led to the floor above. "Sorry about that. I usually take them off by the door, but I don't have to."

Deborah stepped away from the dried mud lying in clumps on the floor where the boots had been. With one hand she lifted her cream-colored silk skirt a couple of inches and hoped there were no more piles of dirt. She looked around. Although the floor looked as if it needed to be swept, the dirt was at least spread thin over the rest of the large room that appeared to be parlor, kitchen, and dining room all in one.

An open door to her left revealed a bedroom. The stairway in the back of the big room led upstairs where she assumed there were more bedrooms. She saw an outside door in the back wall of the kitchen.

Letting her gaze return to the parlor, Deborah's heart sank at the job before her. A couch held various articles of clothing. Deborah assumed that was Dane's clean laundry since dirty clothing littered the floor from the bedroom door into the kitchen.

Dane set Tommy down and said, "I'll carry in the food from the wagon before a stray animal decides to have supper."

Before Deborah could answer, he slipped out the door with Tommy toddling after him. She let them go and clutching Beth close, stepped over dirty clothing, tools, and even a saddle on her way to the kitchen. A closer look there showed dirty dishes that would have to be washed before they could eat supper.

No wonder he'd been eager to run outside while she looked around. She sighed. She couldn't do it overnight, but in a few days she would have a clean house to live in. Dane didn't seem to be overbearing like her father and Jamison had been. His main concern seemed to be for his children. As long as she kept the house and took care of the children, he would likely leave her alone just as he had suggested. She would be free for the first time in her life.

Why, then, did she feel a sense of something missing? Why did she keep remembering the kiss Dane had given her at the close of their wedding ceremony? Why did she want another?

She picked her way across the floor to the door at the other end. She would do well to forget Dane and his kisses and concentrate on the opportunity that had been handed to her. As Dane's wife she would have the children she longed for without the danger and discomfort of giving birth. She would have a home of her own to care for without an overbearing man criticizing her every move—at least she hoped Dane would not turn out to be like Jamison.

She stepped into the bedroom and laid the sleeping baby in the crib that stood beside the four-poster double bed. She gave her a pat and backed out of the room as Dane and Tommy came in from outdoors.

Dane carried a large box. "Where do you want this? Looks like there's everything from meat dishes to desserts in here."

Deborah closed the door and stepped around and over the littered floor to the kitchen table. She marveled that Dane didn't trip on anything as he followed her. "I'll clear a space for it."

Dane waited without a word until she had the corner clean enough for him to set the box down. At the very least, Jamison would have complained about the heavy box. She mentally reprimanded herself for thinking ill of the dead.

"I'll go take care of the horses now." Dane picked up his son. "You want to go with me, Tommy?"

"Yes." The little boy nodded.

"I'll have supper ready by the time you get back." Deborah watched them go back out the front door, then turned toward the dirty dishes.

She was glad to find some warm water on the cookstove and soon had a dishpan of soapy water. She couldn't wash them all, but she determined to make a dent in the pile before she set out their food.

❧

Dane unhitched the team and took care of their needs while his little boy watched, chattering endlessly about one thing and another. He didn't listen and didn't figure Tommy cared as long as he nodded and said "Uh-huh" at the right times. His mind was on the woman in his house.

Deborah hadn't liked the mess she found when she stepped through the door. He should have thought and cleaned it up. After Anne died he'd let things go. There never seemed to be time for everything, and the house kept getting dirty, anyway.

He wandered around in the barn, finding things to do that didn't need to be done until he figured he'd run out of time. He milked the cow and picked up the full pail. Might as well go in and face the disappointment he'd already seen in her eyes. As he and Tommy walked past the corner of the barn, Dane saw a couple of tiny white flowers with yellow centers growing just off the path. He stopped on impulse and picked them. Holding them out of sight, he opened the door to the house and let Tommy go in first.

While Tommy held Deborah's attention, Dane poured water in a glass as if he were going to take a drink but slipped the flowers in instead. He set the tiny bouquet on the table that he noticed was now cleaned off and shining.

He stepped back to watch while Deborah set a dish of potato salad on the table. He knew when she saw the flowers by the way she stopped and her eyes widened.

She turned with a smile. He liked the way her dark eyes lit up when she smiled. "How pretty and thoughtful. Thank you."

He shrugged, but her praise warmed his heart. After Dane

prayed, Tommy kept the conversation going as he told of helping his daddy with the horses. Which was just as well. Dane couldn't have thought of anything to say if he'd tried. He found that he liked Deborah's smile, though, and wished he could bring another to her face.

When they finished eating, he leaned back in his chair and patted his stomach. "That was mighty good for a change."

Deborah looked up at him. "I can't take credit since the food was already cooked."

Dane grinned. "Maybe not, but you didn't burn anything heating it up, either. This is the first meal we've had at this table for ages that didn't have a charcoal taste."

His reward was a bubble of laugher from Deborah.

seven

Deborah slipped into the big bed alone and smiled. How wondrously different from her first wedding night. Dane had taken Tommy to the outhouse, and then he'd locked the door while Tommy scampered up the stairs to the floor above. With no more than a gruff good night, her new husband had left her standing alone in the sitting room and climbed upstairs after his son.

She blew the light out and lay back to stare into the blackness of her strange, new bedroom. Hers and Beth's. As she thought of the baby, her smile widened. Tommy might remember his mother, but Beth would have no memories of any mother but Deborah. Now, away from Mrs. Stark, she could begin being the mother to Beth and Tommy that she wanted to be. Cora Stark was a wonderful woman, but Deborah hadn't felt free under her watchful eye to act as more than a sitter for the children. She felt strangely content with her new life and, at the same time, felt angry and hurt by her father for his high-handed ways of forcing her to marry a man she didn't know. She closed her eyes as sleep claimed her body.

Deborah felt as if she had no sooner lay down than the baby's wail brought her to a groggy awareness. She had never heard Beth cry so—as if she were in terrible pain. Deborah stumbled from bed and with fumbling fingers lit the lamp. In the soft light she saw the baby's arms and legs waving while the high-pitched crying continued. She scooped her new daughter up and wrapped the blanket around her to hold her close.

"Poor baby," she crooned while she patted Beth's back. "You are freezing. No wonder you are crying."

Deborah walked the floor patting the baby while she held her close, hoping her body heat would warm her. But Beth was not so easily consoled. She continued crying, her tiny body tense, her arms and legs thrashing.

Deborah didn't understand. The night was not that cold. She held one miniature arm in her hand and realized that she was no longer cold. What then could be the matter?

When she heard the stairs to the floor above creak, she knew that Dane had been awakened. Maybe he would know what to do. She opened the door and stepped out into the larger room. Dane didn't even glance her way as he carried a lamp to the kitchen table and set it down. He lifted a damp cloth from a crock sitting near the back door, dipped milk out, and poured it into a bottle. Then he fitted a rubber nipple over the end and set it in a pan of water already warming on the stove.

Deborah watched him and felt heat course through her body. No one had told her that Beth needed to eat at night. Dane acted so sure as if he knew how to stop the crying. Deborah took the bottle he handed her and offered the nipple to Beth. She latched on and sucked as if she were starving.

Deborah looked up and found Dane watching her. She sank into a rocking chair in the sitting room, holding the baby against her as a shield when she realized she wore only her flannel nightgown. Although it covered her completely, she still felt undressed before him. That and her incompetence unnerved her.

"She gets hungry in the middle of the night." Dane spoke as his gaze shifted from his daughter.

Deborah met his gaze, knowing he would think her totally stupid. "I'm sorry. I didn't know that. I've never been around babies before."

He grinned, the whiteness of his teeth flashing in the dim light. "Yeah, I think you mentioned something about that earlier today. If you're all right with her, I'll head on back to bed."

"Yes, we're fine." She stood and walked toward the bedroom door.

"Good." He went to the kitchen table and picked up his lamp before starting upstairs. His voice stopped her at the door. "The bottles are in that cabinet there over the milk. She'll want another one early in the morning."

She turned around and saw him standing at the foot of the stairs. He had pulled his clothes on before coming downstairs, but had not buttoned his shirt. The intimacy of the situation set her pulse racing. She stepped into the bedroom. "Thank you."

Deborah could not get Dane out of her mind and lay awake long after Beth slept. The early morning sun had just touched her window when Beth's cry woke her. Knowing what caused the screams this time, she smoothed the baby's blankets in passing and went into the kitchen to fix a bottle. With almost every other dish dirty, Deborah was amazed to find a clean bottle. Obviously Dane realized the importance of keeping a supply handy.

Just as she headed back to the bedroom with the warmed bottle, Tommy started down the stairs. Deborah hesitated. Beth screamed as if she were in terrible pain. "Tommy, do you need help on the stairs?"

"No."

That was plain enough, but what if he fell? He was only two years old, and he had on some sort of a nightshirt. What if he stepped on the tail and tripped? She started up the stairs.

"No." Tommy backed away from her, and Beth's screams sounded even louder.

Deborah was sure Tommy would fall, but she needed to feed Beth. Where was Dane?

"Stay right there, Tommy. Don't come down yet." Deborah hurried into the bedroom, hoping Tommy would obey. She picked up the baby, blanket and all, trying to ignore the soaked diaper, and went back into the big room.

Tommy had descended several more steps. Deborah stuck the nipple in Beth's mouth, but the baby didn't seem to realize it was there. She continued screaming, and Tommy went down another step. His hand barely touched the railing. He teetered before regaining his balance. Deborah had both hands full with the baby and didn't know what to do. She ran up the stairs to stand in front of Tommy.

"No." He pushed at her. "Me do."

Deborah backed down a couple of steps. All right, she'd let him do it himself, but she'd stand ready to block his fall. She brushed the nipple against Beth's lips, moving it back and forth until the baby latched on. The silence almost deafened her. She continued down the stairs a step ahead of Tommy and breathed again when he reached the ground floor.

Why had she thought she could be a mother to two babies? She knew nothing about them. She lowered herself and Beth into the rocker as she relaxed her trembling limbs. Where was Dane, anyway?

Tommy bounced in front of her and then ran through the room to the back door. He probably thought his father had gone outside. She would gladly let Dane take over the responsibility of his son, but she couldn't let him out when she didn't know where Dane was, and she couldn't go looking for him until Beth finished her bottle.

"No, Tommy, we have to stay inside now."

Tommy ran back and straddled the saddle that still sat on the floor. He played while Beth finished eating. Deborah stood and went back into the bedroom. She needed to get dressed before Dane showed up. Beth's bright blue eyes looked up at her as if trying to recognize her. Deborah smiled and after a quick kiss on the baby's forehead, laid her in the middle of her bed.

Tommy pushed the door open as Deborah slipped her dress over her head. For just a moment she thought Dane had come in and her heart pounded. Then her head came through, and she saw Tommy looking up at her as if he wondered what she might be doing in his house.

She smiled at the little boy and buttoned the bodice of her dress. "Hey, are you going to help me with breakfast?"

He pranced around her saying, "Me go. . . ."

She couldn't understand the last word. "You go where?"

He ran through the house with her following. Again he went to the back door and tried to open it. "Tommy, I don't understand, but if you are looking for your father—"

The front door opened and Dane walked in. "He isn't looking for me. He needs to go to the outhouse."

Deborah felt as if she had shrunk two feet. In a tiny voice she squeaked, "I didn't know."

Dane ignored her as he grabbed his son and went out the back door. Deborah watched the door block them from sight. How many more times would she be saying "I didn't know"? A hundred? A thousand? How long before Dane realized he had made a mistake in marrying her?

As the baby let out a piercing cry, Deborah's heart jumped into her throat. She had left her on the bed alone. "Please, Lord, don't let her have fallen off the bed."

She ran, jumping over the objects on the floor and burst through the door into the bedroom to find Beth still lying on her back, her arms and legs jerking as she cried. Deborah picked her up and remembered the wet diaper that now gave off a pungent odor. "Oh, baby, I'm sorry. I forgot about your little problem, which is just as well, I suppose, since it seems to have grown into a big problem."

Beth stopped crying and looked into Deborah's eyes as if trying to understand. Deborah smiled and continued talking to the baby. "Let's get you cleaned up. At least that's something I've done before. Maybe I can do something right for a change."

Deborah found a supply of diapers by the crib. She wet a washcloth to clean the baby and soon had her smiling again. She carried the clean, sweet-smelling baby into the other room just as Dane and Tommy came inside. When Dane glanced at the table, she realized he had probably expected breakfast.

"I'm sorry, I haven't had time to cook anything yet. I need to get Tommy dressed and then I can start some oatmeal. That shouldn't take long."

"No, want mine mommy." Tommy stuck his thumb in his mouth and sidled closer to his father.

Deborah looked up at Dane in surprise. Tommy had not mentioned his mother since that first time in the barn. She stood holding Beth, not sure what she should do. She looked for a safe place to put the baby.

Dane stepped forward. "Here, let me take her. I'll get Tommy dressed while you see about something for us to eat."

Deborah relinquished the baby while she fought against the burning in her eyes. She would not give in and cry in front of either Dane or his children. Her emotions seemed so close to the surface, and she didn't know why. Dane had not spoken even one harsh word to her in spite of her ineptitude in caring for his children. Jamison had struck her for less and she hadn't cried. Now here she was, wanting to cry because her husband hadn't yelled at her. Nothing made any sense.

Deborah soon had oatmeal bubbling and bacon frying. At least she knew her way around a kitchen. Dane and Tommy would eat well if nothing else. But what of Beth? Did she eat real food? She couldn't remember Cora giving her anything other than milk. She set the table with dishes she had washed the night before and called Dane and Tommy.

Deborah took Beth so Dane could eat. She sat across the table from him and bowed her head while he prayed. With Beth balanced in one arm, Deborah picked up her spoon. Eating with one hand was not easy, but she managed.

"You could lay her down," Dane suggested.

And have her start crying again? Deborah gave him a tight smile. "This is fine."

Both babies were quiet. While Tommy ate, Beth sat propped against Deborah and watched the others. Dane didn't speak again until he finished eating.

He stood and Tommy scrambled to get down from his chair. "I need to get some plowing done today. I'll be back in about noon."

"Me go wiff you." Tommy ran to the door.

"No, Tommy, you stay here with your new mama." Dane caught the little boy up and set him down well away from the door.

Tommy's face puckered and he wailed. "Mommy. Want mine mommy."

"Oh, great." Dane looked as if he'd like to bolt for the door.

Deborah pushed Dane's clean clothing to the end of the sofa, then laid Beth toward the back and hoped she wouldn't roll off. To make sure, she pulled a handful of the clothing into a pile in front of the baby. Then she turned toward Tommy.

"Hey, Tommy, we'll have fun today while Daddy works. Okay?"

"No." He grabbed his father's hand and held on as if Deborah might pull him away. "Want mine mommy."

Beth added her tearful voice to Tommy's loud cries. Deborah

didn't know which child to go to as their cries reached a deafening level. She feared what might happen if she tried to console either of them. Whatever she tried would probably just make matters worse.

"Hi. Guess I don't have to ask if anyone is home." Lenore opened the door and walked in. She squatted down and held her hands out to Tommy with a wide smile. "Hey, fella, come see Auntie Lenore."

Tommy released his father and ran across the room to Lenore, his tears forgotten. Deborah watched her pick him up and give him a hug before she went to the sofa.

"Well, no wonder you're crying, precious." She sat on the edge of the sofa and, with Tommy on her lap, picked up Beth and patted her back, all the time crooning nonsense to her about the cruelty of being stuffed into the corner and left. Deborah felt that each word she spoke was meant as criticism toward her, but she ignored Lenore and met Dane's gaze.

In the sudden quiet, his voice sounded loud. "I'll go milk the cow while you get the kids settled down, and then I've got to get to work."

As he went out the back door, Lenore looked up from the little ones and made a sound of disgust. "Anne milked the cow and gave birth to the children, too."

Deborah wondered what she had done to deserve Lenore's scorn. This morning had been rough, and she hadn't known what to do. That was true. But she would learn and the little ones would adjust to her in time. Although if she did what she wanted to do at the moment, she would be out the door and on her way back home to her mother before Dane ever missed her. She didn't know whether to laugh or cry as she remembered the look on Dane's face. Too many more mornings like this one and he would be taking her all the way back to St. Louis himself.

eight

Deborah turned away from the door and her longing to walk through it. Tommy sat at Lenore's feet playing with something he'd picked up off the floor. Lenore sat in the rocking chair with the baby held close. She didn't act like she planned to leave anytime soon, but maybe it wouldn't hurt to ask.

"I'm sorry things were in such an uproar when you stopped." Deborah tried to smile. "Did you need something, or were you just passing by and heard the racket?"

"Oh, no." Lenore laughed. "I started out to my mother's. She lives a couple of miles up the creek. When I saw Dane's house, I thought it would be the neighborly thing to stop in and see if I could help with anything. Seein' as you're new, you know."

No, she didn't know. She had a week's worth of cleaning staring her in the face. She didn't have time to entertain company now. Besides, she had hoped to spend some time alone with Dane's children. How could they ever look to her as their mother if someone else always took care of them?

"That's very nice of you." Deborah picked her words carefully, trying to sound gracious. "As you can see, I've got my work cut out for me, though. I can't think of a thing I need right now more than time and elbow grease."

Lenore laughed again. "Don't let me stop you. If you want to clean Dane's mess up, you go right ahead. I'll play with Tommy and Beth for a while. We always have so much fun when we're together. Don't we, little angel?"

Lenore turned her attention to the baby, playing with

her hands, talking nonsense and laughing at Beth's facial expressions. Deborah stared at her and then shrugged. Beth seemed happy enough. Tommy, too. She should be thankful to have a few minutes without the children underfoot. Maybe she could get some cleaning done if she ignored the trio in her sitting room. It was worth a try. She headed toward the kitchen with resolute steps.

By the time the dishes were washed, Deborah knew she wouldn't have the luxury of ignoring Lenore. Already she had heard more than she wanted to know about how Dane and Anne had met.

"We all grew up here together. Dane, Billy, Anne, me—and Wesley. That's Dane's brother. You haven't met him yet. We're all terribly worried about him since he hasn't come home from the war yet." Lenore walked with the baby into the kitchen while Deborah tackled the sitting room floor. She found a large basket in the corner and started filling it with dirty clothing.

"Billy and Dane, of course, are cousins. We went to school together. You can't imagine how ornery Dane was."

Deborah straightened and stared at Lenore. She tried to picture Dane dipping Lenore's dark braids in the inkwell or stealing a kiss behind the schoolhouse and couldn't. Surely Lenore was making up most of the stories she told. Otherwise Dane must have been in love with Lenore when he married Anne. The walk home from school, the parties, running off to go fishing together, even her first kiss had come from Dane. Maybe she had Dane and Wesley confused.

Deborah went back to work when Lenore took Beth into the bedroom to change her diaper. Tommy trailed after her, saying he had to go to the outhouse. Deborah understood him perfectly that time, but she ignored him, letting Lenore handle the problem. She stuffed the last article of clothing in the basket and set it to the side. Already the place looked better. She went into the kitchen to check on the bread that she had set out to rise earlier.

A glance out the window showed that the sun had already moved past midmorning. Dane would want his noon meal soon. She punched the dough down and shaped it into loaves. She still had enough leftover dishes from their wedding for lunch, so she didn't have to worry about cooking anything except bread. She went back into the sitting room and started sorting the clean clothing on the sofa while Lenore took Tommy outside.

She could hear the baby cooing in the crib. She laid the shirt she had just picked up on Dane's pile and went to check on her. She tiptoed into the bedroom, feeling as if she were trespassing and might be caught at any moment. But that was ridiculous. This was her house now—certainly not Lenore's. The two children were her stepchildren, not Lenore's.

Her heart softened at the sight of little Beth lying on her back, her hands held up in front of her face. As Deborah watched, the baby's eyes drifted closed and her arms slowly relaxed until they rested at either side of her head.

Deborah jumped and turned back to the sitting room when the back door opened. She faced Lenore and, in spite of herself, explained, "I was just checking on Beth. She's asleep."

"Yes, I knew she would be." Lenore's superior attitude grated on Deborah's nerves.

The thought of shoving her visitor back out the door and locking it flitted through Deborah's mind. Of course, she would never try such a thing. But the fantasy made her feel a little better.

"Where do you live, Lenore?" She tried polite conversation instead.

"Ours is the next house to the west. We live just across the creek from Billy's mother. Most folks built along Cedar Creek at first to be near water before they dug wells. Dane's folks had their own supply with that spring there at the edge of the woods. Did Dane take you down to see it?"

Deborah shook her head. "No, I've only been here a week and kept pretty busy then."

A smile spread Lenore's lips. "He took me a few times." A soft giggle escaped. "It's mighty pretty there. Romantic, if you know what I mean."

No, but she had a good idea. Deborah turned her back toward Lenore to set out the food she needed to warm for lunch. She made a face and wished she had the nerve to tell Lenore to go home. Maybe their marriage wasn't real, but she'd still like to spend some time with Dane so that they could become friends. And the children—how could she become a mother to them if she couldn't get near them?

Deborah set three plates on the table, hoping Lenore would get the message. She should have known better. Lenore didn't seem to notice, and when Dane came through the back door, Billy Reid followed him inside.

"Figured I'd find you here." He frowned at his wife.

Deborah waited, hoping he would take Lenore and go home.

"I've been helping Deborah get settled in." Lenore swept a hand out to show the much neater room, as if she had done the work herself.

"That's real nice of you, Lenore. Are you and Billy stayin' for dinner?" Dane turned to Deborah then, as if just remembering her. "There's plenty left over from the dinner yesterday, isn't there?"

"Sure, we'll stay." Billy stepped to the table all the time keeping his gaze on Deborah. A slow grin settled across his handsome face. "If the food's as good as the cook looks, then we can't go wrong."

"Oh, Billy." Lenore smacked his arm. "She's just warming it up. She didn't cook anything."

Deborah opened the oven door and slid a pan of golden-brown bread out. She turned the loaf upside down on a platter and then righted it to spread butter over the top.

"Don't reckon that came from the leftovers." Billy winked at Deborah. "Looks real good, angel."

"Her name's Deborah." Lenore turned to smile at Dane. "So your wife said you were plowing. Are you getting ready to plant corn?"

Deborah listened to Dane and Lenore talk about the crops he would be putting in. She knew little about farming and didn't understand everything they said. Or maybe her mind wasn't on the conversation. Billy kept looking at her and grinning as if they had a secret. Dane didn't seem to notice. Or if he did, he didn't care. She was glad when they finished eating. Maybe now Billy and Lenore would leave.

"Guess I'd better get back to the field. I'll be plowing all week and need to put in as much time as I can while it's light." Dane pushed back from the table. He looked directly at Deborah for the first time since he'd come in. "You might want to go ahead and fix supper for Tommy and yourself at the usual time. Just leave some out for me, if you don't mind. I probably won't be in until dark."

"All right." She nodded and couldn't help wondering if he planned to stay outside to avoid her.

When Dane stood and headed toward the door, Tommy scrambled out of his chair and followed him. "Me go, too. Me go wiff you, Daddy."

"Tommy, I can't take you out in the field." Dane looked across the room at Deborah in a silent plea for help.

She stepped forward. "Tommy—"

"I'll take him out for a while." Lenore stepped in front of

Deborah. "We were so busy inside that he didn't get to go out and play."

"Thanks, Lenore." Dane didn't look at Deborah again as he went out the door.

"I'll get your jacket, Tommy, and then we'll go outside," Lenore promised as she hurried across the floor.

Deborah didn't realize where she was going until she started up the stairs. Her heart sank. She hadn't had time to clean upstairs yet. Lenore had already been in her bedroom. If she had looked, she'd seen all of Deborah's things in there and none of Dane's. Now she would see Dane's and Tommy's clothing and know where each of them had slept.

Her face flushed as she turned away to clear the table. There was nothing she could do now except hope that Lenore didn't snoop. Billy followed her around the table before he pulled out a chair and sat in it.

"Lenore's in love with Dane, you know."

"What?" Deborah swung around, almost dropping the glasses she clutched in her hands.

"Always has been. Dane, too." Billy shrugged but looked none too happy. "Don't know why Dane married Anne. But, soon as he did, Lenore said she'd marry me. I thought she'd get over him. Never has, though. Nor him her. Guess you saw how cozy they were, talkin' about puttin' in the crops."

She'd seen but hadn't thought anything about it. Then Lenore's stories of her and Dane walking out and meeting behind the school and at the spring came back to her. But it didn't matter. None of it did. Because she and Dane didn't have a normal marriage. She couldn't feel threatened when she had nothing to lose. So what if Dane loved Lenore? He would never love her anyway.

She smiled at Billy around the hurt that didn't make sense. "Even if what you say is true, it doesn't matter. Maybe something did go on between them, but that was a long time ago. Lenore married you, and I'm sure she has come to love you very much."

Billy grinned, his good nature seemingly in place again. "You're a catch, you know that? Poor ol' Dane probably didn't have any idea what he got when he married you."

Deborah stared at Billy and wondered what trouble he was trying to stir up. She was almost glad for the interruption when Lenore clambered down the stairs, Tommy's jacket in her hand.

She laughed as she helped Tommy put his jacket on. "Did you get scared all by yourself last night, Tommy, so Daddy had to stay with you?"

Tommy didn't seem to understand, or he didn't hear as he chattered about going outside. But Deborah did, and if the gleam in Lenore's eyes and the smirk on her face was any indication, she knew that Deborah understood.

* * *

Deborah breathed a sigh of relief when Lenore and Billy left an hour later. Lenore had insisted on putting Tommy down for his nap, and Deborah didn't argue. Now, with Beth lying on a folded quilt on the floor playing with her hands, she headed to the kitchen.

Dane probably thought Lenore had helped clean the house. Deborah turned and looked at the large room that served as both sitting room and kitchen. She hadn't had time to sweep and mop the floor like she wanted to, but she had picked up most of the clutter and she'd folded and put away the clean clothes. The house looked much better, although there was still plenty to do.

She turned back to her next project. She wanted to bake something special for Dane. Thanks to Lenore and Billy the dishes from their wedding dinner were empty. She stirred up the fire and set the teakettle of water on the stove to warm then rummaged in Dane's supplies until she pulled out a container of dried apple slices.

A tendril of hair fell across her face as she readied the pan to wash dishes, and she brushed it back. The kitchen was too warm, but she needed the fire if she was going to bake an apple pie with the dried apples. With summer just around the corner, she wondered how she would be able to cook then. She thought of her mother's summer kitchen and realized what a luxury it had been.

By the time Tommy woke from his nap, Deborah had the dishes washed and the pie sitting on the pie safe cooling. She ran upstairs when she heard Tommy moving around.

"Hi. Are you ready to get up?"

Tommy sat in the middle of the bed, rubbing his eyes. When he lifted his head, Deborah saw the pucker and knew what was coming. A wail erupted with the barely distinguishable words, "Want mine mommy."

"Oh, Tommy." Deborah sat on the edge of the bed and took the little boy in her arms. He resisted at first, but she held him close, patting his back as if he were Beth. "It's all right, baby. I'm sorry I'm not your real mama. But I'm here and I'll do the best I can to fill in for her."

About the time Deborah's own lashes grew moist, Tommy stopped crying and pulled away. He climbed from her lap and headed to the stairs, dragging a small quilt behind him. Deborah followed.

Tommy didn't mention his mother again that afternoon, but he stayed as far from Deborah as he could, ignoring her overtures of friendship. He lay on his tummy and played with Beth, keeping her occupied while Deborah fixed their supper of sweet potatoes and peas with a couple of slices of side meat. She cut thin slices from the second loaf of bread she had baked that morning and set a place for Tommy at the table. She decided she would wait for Dane. Maybe their marriage wasn't real, but they still needed to function like a family, and she was getting tired of being ignored by both Tommy and Dane.

While Tommy ate, Deborah fed Beth and wondered about the vegetables in Dane's pantry. Did he have a garden? She had helped her mother with their small garden plot and had always enjoyed watching the plants grow. Surely tomorrow Lenore would stay away, and she could get outside to see what she could find.

When the house grew dark, Deborah lit the lamp in the sitting room. Tommy and Beth were both asleep in their beds when Dane came in the back door. His gaze swept the room, and Deborah thought he stiffened for a moment when he saw her sitting on the end of the sofa.

"Your supper is ready." Deborah stood and went to the kitchen where she set a plate for each of them on the table.

"Thanks." Dane washed his hands and dried them on the towel hanging above the basin. "You didn't have to wait up."

Don't you mean to say "I wish you hadn't waited up"? Deborah smiled. "I didn't mind. The children have already eaten and are asleep. This will give us time to get acquainted."

"Yeah, I guess so."

Deborah bowed her head while Dane prayed. She knew he felt as strange as she did, sitting across from her. This was the first time they had been alone since they had met. They ate in silence for a few minutes. Then Deborah asked, "Did you get a lot done?"

He looked up at her as if he had forgotten she was there. "More than usual. It helps not having to make the trip to get the kids." The hint of a smile touched his face. "Pretty nice to not have to wrestle them to bed, too."

"I imagine." Tommy had wanted to stay up, but he'd gone to his bed easily enough when Deborah had suggested she rock him to sleep. It still hurt that he'd rather go off alone to his bedroom than let her hold him.

They talked while they ate. Not a real conversation, but Deborah was content. All she wanted was to be friends with Dane. Yet, after he locked the house and went upstairs, Deborah stopped by the mirror in her room, and before she could control her thoughts, she wondered if Dane found her pretty.

nine

One month later in June, Dane asked Deborah, "Would you like to go to Ivy?"

When she just stared at him, he grinned. "It's a little settlement named after my aunt Ivy. We could drop the kids off with Lenore on the way."

He watched a frown touch her face. She probably didn't care for Lenore any more than he did, but Tommy seemed to think a lot of Lenore. That meant she treated the kids well, and she always seemed to like watching them.

"I thought you might like to mail a letter to your folks. Ivy's got a post office."

Deborah smiled then. "Yes, I would like to write to my mother. How soon do you plan to leave?"

He shrugged and picked up Tommy. "Soon as you get a letter written, I reckon. We'll be outside. Just let me know when you're ready."

He headed toward the barn. Might as well hitch up the team. The corn was planted, and he figured Deborah deserved an outing and a break from taking care of the kids. She'd done wonders with the house. Seemed almost like a home again. After Anne died, he'd gone through each day doing only what had to be done. Was Beth only three months old? Seemed like a lot longer since Anne died.

He hadn't said much about the house being clean and having three good meals on the table each day, but he appreciated Deborah's efforts. Beth already cried for her when anyone else tried to take her, just like she was Beth's own mother. Tommy hadn't been so quick to take to her, but he had started letting her do things for him. Wouldn't be long before she won him over, too.

"Hey, you wanna go for a ride?"

Tommy nodded. "Yes."

Dane set his small son up on Old Dobbin's wide back and grinned at his "Gettyup!"

Holding Tommy steady with one hand, Dane led the big horse to the buckboard. He moved Tommy to the back of the wagon while he hitched up the horse, then drove to the house, stopping near the front door. He set the brake and secured the reins then reached for his son.

"Let's go see if Mama's ready."

He'd been afraid to call Deborah "Mama" at first, using "your new mama" instead. But the last few days, he'd started referring to her as "Mama" and Tommy hadn't seemed to mind. Tommy was little, but Dane knew he remembered Anne. His prayer was for Deborah to fill the void left in Anne's absence but not take her memory completely from Tommy. Yet Dane wondered how long it would be before Tommy's memory of his mother would be centered on the one tintype of her that they had.

Deborah had Beth dressed and was finishing her letter when Dane and Tommy went back inside. She stood with a smile. "Looks like you two are ready to go and so are we."

Dane couldn't tear his gaze from her face. She seemed prettier now than she had the first time he'd seen her. The difference, he thought, was in her eyes. They'd shown fear before. Fear and maybe anger. He understood that. From what she'd said, her father had pretty much forced her into marrying him. Maybe he should have put a stop to the whole thing, but he hadn't known what else to do. His kids needed a mother. And from what he'd seen in the last month, he couldn't have made a better choice if he'd had a whole bevy of girls to choose from.

Besides, there wasn't any fear or anger in her eyes this morning. They sparkled with excitement. He grinned. She probably thought Ivy was something worth seeing.

"Yeah, we're ready, but we didn't intend to hurry you."

She picked Beth up. "You didn't. I finished my letter. Can I get a stamp there?"

He nodded. "Should be able to at the post office."

He took Beth and held her in one arm while he helped Deborah climb onto the buckboard seat. As soon as she straightened her skirts around her, she took the baby. Dane swung Tommy up to sit beside her and then he climbed on and took up the reins.

It didn't take long to get to Billy and Lenore's house. Dane took the kids in while Deborah waited outside. Lenore seemed eager to watch the kids, and Tommy ran through the house with no more than a wave and a good-bye. Dane gave Beth a quick kiss, handed her to Lenore, and hurried back out to the buckboard.

"That didn't take long." Deborah seemed to hesitate before she allowed a smile to curve her lips.

Dane snapped the reins and they moved out. "Tommy went running off to get into who-knows-what, so I handed Beth to Lenore and left before she changed her mind."

Deborah's soft laughter touched a cord in Dane's heart. He felt comfortable with her sitting beside him—as if she should be there—and hoped she felt the same way. They didn't talk much on the drive to Ivy, but the silence rested him. He glanced at her as they approached the tiny town.

"There she is. I told you it wasn't much."

Deborah looked from side to side as they drove down the only street. A scattering of homes sandwiched the businesses that lined the street on either side. Dane pulled to a stop in front of Ivy's general store. Deborah turned to him with a smile. "It may not be much, but besides the store you have a blacksmith and a feed store. And no saloon. That's good."

Dane grinned. "Nope. Some have tried, but Aunt Ivy won't stand for it. Since she still holds the deed to this land, she has the say in what goes in here."

"Imagine owning a town."

Dane laughed. "Imagine anyone in my family owning a town. Aunt Ivy's about the only one who has the ambition to do more than farm. Billy sure didn't inherit her drive."

Dane climbed down and walked around to help Deborah. In the store, the proprietor, Tom Jordan, stood behind the high counter talking to a local farmer and the area doctor. Dane spoke to them and handed the list of needed supplies to Tom. "Here's what we need, and we want to check on any mail. My wife's got a letter to mail out to her folks, too."

"Yeah, I heard ya got married again." Tom turned to Deborah. "Glad to meet you, ma'am. If you'll come back here, we'll check on that mail for you first."

Dane started to follow Deborah, but Harley Sinclair stopped him. "Hey, Dane, you had any trouble out your way?"

"Trouble?" He looked from one man to the other.

Doc Lewis nodded. "Yeah, seems the area's been visited by bushwhackers here lately."

"I thought the war was over." Dane glanced at Deborah in the back of the store. She looked up and met his gaze with a hesitant smile. He didn't want her worrying about something like this.

Harley shrugged. "You know well as I do that an outlaw don't clean up his act just because his excuse for raidin' other people's property is gone. Word is that a couple of farms west of here lost some tools and some food. Neither family was home when it happened."

"Might be a good idea to lock up whatever you can if you're going to be gone, especially after dark." Doc Lewis shook his head. "The war brought a lot of changes to our country, didn't it? And not all of them good."

"Yeah, I reckon so. Thanks for letting me know about this." Dane watched Deborah turn and browse through the store. As she headed their way, a strong desire to protect her rose in his heart. He decided a change of topic was in order. "I just finished puttin' in my corn. If the weather holds out, I should have a good crop."

As he had hoped, the other two launched into a discussion of farming and the weather. As Deborah drew close he stepped to her side. "Did you find anything you'd like to have?"

Deborah looked up at him as if she didn't understand. "The shopkeeper has the list."

"I mean something for you. Maybe some cloth for a new dress?" He pointed at the bolts of fabric where she had been looking.

"I don't have to have anything."

Anne had never turned down a gift. Dane wondered at Deborah's hesitation. "You've been doing a great job with the kids and the house. I'd like to give you something special as a sort of wedding present. Why don't you go see if any of that cloth catches your fancy?"

A shy smile relaxed her lips. "If you're sure it's all right."

"I'm sure." He placed a hand on each of her shoulders and turned her in the right direction, then gave a gentle push.

She giggled as she walked away. Dane liked her giggle. As a matter of fact, he liked Deborah. Maybe too much. They'd been married only a month, and he found it harder each day to keep his mind, and his hands, off her. How could he continue to keep his distance with her slowly but surely making a place for herself in his home and in his heart? When Anne died he'd retreated into a protective shell where there was no feeling. No laughter or happiness. In the past month he'd found his way to the edge of that shell where he could peek out once in a while and laugh with Deborah. He turned back to the front counter to check over his purchases while Tom helped Deborah cut a length of cloth from the bolt she had selected.

❧

Deborah stood to the side while Dane paid for their supplies; then she walked ahead of him outside to the buckboard. She hadn't expected to get fabric for a new dress. Jamison had never bought her a gift during their courtship or during their marriage. She'd been married to Dane now almost as long as she and Jamison were married. Funny how the two weeks she'd spent with Jamison had seemed like a year. This past month had flown by. Maybe that was because of the little ones. She already loved them as if they were her own.

She held Dane's hand as he helped her climb to the high seat. Dane was such a gentleman even when they were alone. Jamison had been a gentleman in public. Deborah closed her eyes a moment. Why was she comparing the two men? She already knew that Jamison would come up short.

"Is there anything else you want to see while we're here?" Dane picked up the reins and waited for her answer.

Deborah glanced from one end of the street to the other and laughed. Dane's laughter blended with hers. "In that case, why don't we go have our picnic lunch?"

"Yes, I'd like that." Deborah checked to see if the covered basket she had placed under the seat was still there.

Dane drove just outside of town before pulling over to stop under the sheltering branch of an ancient oak tree growing near the side of the road. The dense foliage above provided ample shade to cool and protect them from the warm sun.

"Do you want to get out and spread a quilt on the ground, or would you rather sit in the back of the wagon?" Dane left the decision to Deborah.

Deborah thought of the insects that would soon cover their food on the ground and said, "Is it all right if we stay in the wagon?"

"Sure is." Dane jumped down. "Let me get Old Dobbin's lunch and I'll be right with you."

While Dane fed his horse, Deborah moved some things out of the way and spread the quilt on the floor of the wagon. She dug the basket from under the seat and set it in the middle of the quilt. Feeling like a young girl on an outing with her best beau, she sat cross-legged on the quilt and watched Dane climb aboard.

He sat across from her while she pulled the cover from the basket and took out cold fried potatoes and bacon, a bowl of leftover brown beans, and an apple pie. When she set the pie to the side, she noticed that his eyes lit up, and she smiled. Dane didn't often comment on her cooking, but he always ate his share. She handed him a plate and fork.

After Dane prayed, Deborah waited for him to fill his plate, and then she dipped out her own food.

"Wonder how Lenore's getting along with the kids," Dane said.

"Probably just fine." Deborah hadn't intended to sound so unconcerned and spiteful. The truth was, she had been missing the little ones ever since Dane came out of Lenore's house without them. But she knew they were all right because of the way Tommy always ran to Lenore when he saw her. Lenore would be a good mother. Deborah wondered why the Reids didn't have children then decided it was none of her business.

"I'm sorry," she apologized for her hateful tone of voice. "I just hope she isn't getting along so well with them that they don't want to come home."

Dane looked at Deborah as if trying to see inside her mind. "You don't think Tommy still has a problem, do you? I know he didn't take to you right off, but I thought he'd got used to you by now."

"He cried for his mother at first, but he hasn't done that for a week or so." She smiled at Dane. "I think he likes me all right. I'm just not his mother."

Dane seemed to concentrate on his food for several bites before he looked at her again. "I know you didn't want to marry me and take on my kids. I guess if I'd known what else to do, I'd have put a stop to it before you got all tangled up in my problems."

"Wait." Deborah lay a hand on his arm. "Don't apologize. You are right that I didn't have much choice in the matter, but you must understand that I chose to marry you. That first week at your folks' house, I could see that you were hurting and you needed help, but I saw something even more important than that."

When he just looked at her, a question in his eyes, she continued. "I saw that you were different from either my father or my late husband. I didn't want to go back home and live under my father's roof. He's a good man, but I've always felt bound by his firm rule. I've never been able to live in the freedom I have found here with your family."

"What about your husband?"

Deborah lowered her gaze to her hand still resting on Dane's arm. She jerked her hand back while warmth flooded her cheeks. How could she have sat there touching him, and why had he let her?

"Deborah, how am I different from your first husband?"

Dane repeated the question.

She met his gaze. "Jamison ruled with an iron hand."

"Did he ever hit you?" Suspicion glittered in Dane's blue eyes.

Deborah shrugged. "Only once."

"How long were you together?"

"Two weeks."

Dane made an indistinguishable sound of disgust. "A man who hits a woman, or in any way hurts her, should be horsewhipped."

"Thank you, Dane," Deborah whispered as she fought the tears that threatened at his gentleness. He would be so easy to fall in love with. But she couldn't. She just couldn't fall in love with a man who didn't want her.

"I reckon we'd better be getting back." Dane started picking up and putting the food away.

Deborah couldn't stop the giggle that came partly from his actions and partly from her own raw emotions. "That's exactly what I mean. Jamison and my father would never have cleaned up after a meal."

Dane grinned. "I think we need to forget Jamison."

Deborah sobered as she helped him with the bowls and dishes. "I agree. So why don't you tell me instead about the bushwhackers."

"Bushwhackers?" His hands froze in place.

She nodded. "I heard part of what those men were telling you. Are we in some kind of danger?"

ten

Dane's sigh spoke of the seriousness of the problem. "I didn't intend for you to hear. There's no need to worry. I'll take care of you and the little ones."

"Dane." Deborah again placed her hand on his arm. "I need to know if I should be careful when I go outside or when you aren't near the house."

"Yeah, I guess you're right." Dane put his hand over hers and held it in place. Then he told her all he knew about the reports of roving outlaws taking what they could get from outlying farms in the area. "Just be careful and I think we'll be all right."

She nodded, glad he had trusted her enough to tell her of the danger. When they stopped at Billy and Lenore's, Deborah went with Dane to get the babies.

Billy met them at the door. "Hey, come on in."

Deborah stepped ahead of Dane into the small cabin. Tommy, sitting on the floor near the rocking chair where Lenore sat holding the baby, jumped up and ran to his father. "Daddy, I miss you."

Dane lifted him and gave him a hug. "I missed you, too."

Deborah looked longingly at the little boy. She loved him already and was thankful that he had warmed up to her as much as he had, but she could only dream of the day he would run to her saying he missed her.

"Are you going to give Mama a kiss, too?" At Dane's voice, Deborah held her breath and smiled at the little boy.

He leaned forward with one arm circling her neck and kissed her on the cheek. When he pulled back, he gave her a smile and said, "I miss you."

She moved close to Dane so she could give Tommy a kiss. In just that brief contact with man and boy, Deborah closed her eyes and absorbed the warmth of their presence. She pulled back, knowing she should not open her heart to any more hurt but seemed unable to stop.

Lenore stood to bring Beth to them. As Deborah took the baby, Lenore said, "She's been an angel, as usual. They both have. They are always so good for me."

Deborah cuddled the baby close, ignoring Lenore's insinuations. The children were good for her, too, now that they'd gotten used to her. She smiled at little Beth, getting a sweet baby smile in return.

"We'd better be going." Dane opened the door. "Billy, you gonna walk us out?"

Billy shrugged. "What's up?"

Without answering his cousin, Dane said, "We sure do appreciate you all watching the little ones for us."

"You know we like having them here." Lenore handed Dane a cloth bundle. "I wrapped the soiled diapers in this. The clean ones are still in the satchel you brought."

"Thanks." When Dane took the bundles, Deborah went out to the buckboard. She waited while Dane set Tommy and the bundles in the back of the wagon. He took Beth, then helped Deborah climb aboard. After she took the baby, Dane stepped to the side to speak with Billy. Although he kept his voice low, she could still hear.

Billy's voice carried to her. "The war's over in case you haven't heard."

"Doesn't matter. Some men don't know when to quit. They're outlaws. They don't have a living so they take where they can get it. All I'm saying is that you keep a good lookout and don't let Lenore go out alone."

"So this is about Lenore, is it?"

"What do you mean by that?" Dane's voice rose and Deborah heard each word.

"You always wanted Lenore. Do you think I didn't know that? Ever'body knows it."

"Billy, I have a wife. I'm not interested in yours."

"Hah! You have a housekeeper and that's all." Billy's laugh held no mirth. "So stay away from Lenore."

Deborah's face burned. She turned her attention to the baby in her lap, ignoring the men as Dane spoke in low, serious tones to Billy. How could Billy say those things about her? And how could he think Dane wanted Lenore? She had seen no indication. But what did she know? A small seed of doubt crept into her heart.

Dane climbed onto the seat, taking the reins in his hands. Billy stood watching them leave, but Dane kept his gaze ahead on the short drive home. Deborah didn't know what to expect from her husband because she had never seen him angry before. More than once Jamison had taken his anger out on her, but she sensed that Dane would not. He stopped near the door of the house and climbed down.

At her side, he reached for the baby. "I'll get you in the house, then I'm going to hide our meat. We had to do that during the war sometimes."

"It won't be safe in the smokehouse?"

"No, that's the first place they'll look."

Deborah started a fire in the stove to cook supper while Tommy ran through the house as if making sure everything was still there. She smiled as she watched him run from one thing to another and at last settle on the floor to play with some wooden animals that Dane said his father had carved. Dane didn't come inside until supper was on the table, and then he was quieter than usual.

After supper they put the children to bed, and as if they had agreed, both went back to the kitchen. Deborah filled the coffeepot while Dane sat at the table. "Would you like a slice of cake and some coffee?"

He lifted his head and smiled at her. "That sounds good if you'll have some with me."

Deborah had long been aware of Dane's attractive features, but at that moment when he smiled at her, a melting took place deep in her heart. She turned away on the pretext of putting the coffee on to heat, afraid that her feelings would show in her expression. When she had her flighty emotions under control, she flashed a smile at him. "I was planning to."

"Good."

Deborah cut two slices of cake and set one in front of Dane and the other across the table from him. She set two cups next to the plates, poured their coffee, then sat down.

"Thanks," Dane said. "This is good."

"I'm glad you like it." Deborah hadn't felt so shy around Dane before. In spite of her determination to keep an emotional distance, she felt a special drawing toward him that she had never felt for any other man. Perhaps their outing today without the children had brought them closer together. She hoped so.

"What was your childhood like?" Dane's voice and question surprised her.

Deborah tried to think how to answer his question honestly without sounding as if she were complaining. "My father has always been very strict. When he was home, my brother and I were not allowed to run through the house and play as Tommy does." She smiled, remembering. "However, our mother often let us break the rules when Father was gone. We could not speak at the table. Father's word was law."

"So you married the first time to get away from the restrictions?"

Deborah shook her head. "No. I married because Father told me to."

Dane's eyes widened. "Are you saying—do you mean. . . ?"

She looked down at her coffee. Dane couldn't seem to form the question. She nodded, lifting her gaze to meet his. "I'm saying that this is the second time my father has told me who to marry." She gave a short, bitter laugh. "I'm beginning to think he wanted to get rid of me."

Dane covered her hand with his. She looked into blue eyes soft with compassion. "I'm sorry. I promise you that I didn't know."

"Don't be." She blinked against tears and didn't know why his gentleness upset her more than Jamison's anger had. "I'm glad now that he decided I should marry you and help raise your children. I miss my mother and Caleb, but for the first time in my life, I feel as if I've found a place I can call home. I love Tommy and Beth very much. I hope that's all right."

Dane smiled and lifted her hand to his lips in a soft kiss. "Of course it's all right." He let her hand go as if regretting what he had done. Sadness filled his eyes as he looked across the table at her. "I'm sorry you had to marry me. I can't give you the marriage you deserve, but I promise I'll do everything in my power to make your life easy."

A tear slid down Deborah's cheek before she could stop it. She swiped at it with her hand and tried to smile. Not knowing how to express herself, she stood and picked up their dirty dishes. She rinsed them off and heard Dane scoot his chair back. When she turned around he was gone.

ða

On the Fourth of July, Deborah rose early, anticipating a fun day ahead. Dane's parents had invited them to spend the day visiting and celebrating the holiday. With the war just past, the celebration seemed especially important to Deborah. She left the baby sleeping and went to the kitchen to cook before the sun came up and made the heat unbearable. By the time she had two pies in the oven, Dane came in the back door and went upstairs with no more than a nod in her direction.

Deborah watched him disappear into the bedroom he shared with Tommy. She could hear the low rumble of his voice and Tommy's higher answers. At least he could speak to his son. She turned back to her work, wondering if she had done something to anger him. He had been so gentle and kind the day they'd gone to Ivy. But since then he had seemed to withdraw from her.

They pulled into Cora and Aaron's drive a couple of hours before noon. Deborah allowed Dane to help her climb from the high seat; then she took Beth into the house in search of Cora.

As she went through the front door, Cora called out, "I'm in the kitchen, Deborah."

Dane followed her into the house with the basket of food she had prepared. Cora turned from the stove and smiled at them. "Bless you. Looks like you've brought enough so I can stop cooking right now."

They laughed with her, and Dane set the basket on the table before going back outside where the men were.

Cora watched him leave, then turned to Deborah with a searching gaze. "Dane has looked happier this last month than I've seen him in a long time. I hope that means you two are getting along all right."

Deborah kept her gaze on the dishes she lifted from the basket. "We get along just fine. You can be proud of your son, Mrs. Stark. He's a true gentleman."

"Gentleman?" Cora's eyebrows lifted. Her voice grew solemn. "Deborah, are you happy here?"

This time Deborah had no problem meeting the older

woman's gaze. "Yes, I'm very happy here. I miss my family, but I wouldn't want to go back to St. Louis."

Cora smiled. "Good. Because we certainly wouldn't want you to. You've been my daughter-in-law for two months now. Do you think you could call me something besides Mrs. Stark?"

Deborah had liked Cora from their first meeting. To please her mother-in-law, she would call her whatever she wanted. "What would you like for me to call you?"

"Dane calls me Mom. What do you call your mother?"

"I've always called her Mother."

"Then I would not be taking her name if you called me Mom. Do you think you could do that?"

As tears burned her eyes, Deborah nodded. Her emotions seemed to be on edge all the time anymore. Besides wanting to cry at the least provocation, she had been feeling so tired by the end of the day. She hadn't realized the extent of upheaval moving away from home and marrying a stranger had caused until just the past week when she realized that her monthly hadn't shown up on schedule. Actually, she couldn't remember the last time what with Jamison's death, the war ending, the assassination of President Lincoln, and leaving home to marry Dane. So much had gone on in her life, no wonder her body was reacting.

She smiled at her mother-in-law. "Mom. I think I can do that."

Cora wrapped her in a warm hug, and Deborah blinked to keep the tears at bay. When they pulled back, Cora said, "Let's go outside and see what the men are doing. We need to relax today, too."

Aaron and his sons were playing a game of horseshoes, so Cora and Deborah sat on the porch in the shade and watched. Tommy ran from one uncle to another, soaking up attention while Beth watched with wide-eyed interest from the protection of her grandmother's lap.

Deborah heard several of the family mention Dane's brother, Wesley, who had still not returned from the South where he had fought as a Confederate soldier. Aaron's telegram asking for information had returned saying he was not listed with the casualties, but no one seemed to know where he had disappeared. Without a doubt the family missed him and longed to have him at home.

Dane seemed to enjoy the time with his family. Deborah watched him as they played and teased each other. He laughed, giving as good as he got from his younger brothers. They ate lunch and played again in the afternoon while the babies slept. As Deborah helped Cora set out the warmed leftovers for supper, she felt as if she'd put in a full day's work.

By the time the men had fired a couple of rounds with their rifles to—as Cora said—make as much noise as they could, Deborah could barely keep her eyes open. She was glad when Dane said it was time to go home.

&a.

July and August brought no relief from Dane's busy schedule. Deborah felt the heat more than she ever remembered in St. Louis and wondered if they were really that much farther south. When her time of the month again failed to appear, she became concerned. When frying bacon sent her outside to heave up the contents of her stomach, she wondered.

Her marriage to Jamison had been short, but it had been real. In late August, she stood in the kitchen cleaning up the breakfast dishes. She had managed to keep her sickness each morning from Dane simply because bacon seemed to be the worst offender. Most other odors caused nausea, but not vomiting. And if Dane missed his usual bacon with his eggs, he never mentioned it.

She touched her still-flat stomach and hoped with all her heart that her suspicions were right. If she could not have a real marriage with Dane, she would never have a child of her own. Although she loved Beth and Tommy as if they were hers, she wanted this child very much. But if she was right and there was a child growing inside her womb, she could not tell Dane—at least not yet.

eleven

September brought cooler temperatures as Deborah settled into her life as a farm wife. Dane had never indicated that she should do the milking, and she had no intention of volunteering. From a distance the cows seemed like large, lumbering but gentle animals. Up close, she wasn't so sure how gentle they might be.

The chickens were different. They threw a fit when she stole their eggs, but she didn't mind their hysterics as they flapped their wings and did their funny little running fly across the henhouse while squawking at her. If she took eggs out from under them, they pecked her, but she soon learned to entice them away from the nests with their morning ration of grain first.

Most of her evenings after supper were spent sewing and mending in front of the fireplace. She made a dress to wear to church with the fabric Dane had bought during their trip to Ivy. From the scraps she made a matching dress for Beth and started a rag doll. She worked on the doll after the children had been tucked in bed since it would be a Christmas gift for Beth.

With each passing week, Deborah noticed changes in her body that confirmed her earlier suspicions that she would soon have her own baby. She longed to confide in someone, to ask the multitude of questions that bounced through her mind when she had time to think, but her mother was too far away and she could not go to Cora. She knew she must keep her secret as long as she could because Dane had made it clear that he did not want his wife going through the danger of childbirth. She could only imagine what his reaction would be when he found out she had been with child before they married.

One afternoon in early October, Deborah asked Tommy if he would like to take his nap on a pallet in the sitting room.

"Why?"

She smiled at his usual response to anything new. "Because it's warmer down here than it is upstairs. Besides, I thought you might like to do something different."

Just that morning, Tommy had tried to follow his father outside. Dane didn't see him, and Deborah had to tell him that he couldn't go. Tommy had been just as determined to go with his daddy. When he opened the door, refusing to listen to her, Deborah threatened him with a spanking. She didn't know if she could have carried out her threat, but Tommy believed her and moved away from the door.

He had behaved without a murmur the rest of the morning, and now Deborah wanted to keep him close. She wanted to watch him sleep and know that he was all right. She spread a folded blanket on the floor a short distance from the fireplace where the warmth of the fire would reach him.

"How's this?" She knelt by the pallet and patted the pillow into place then looked at Tommy.

He stood watching her. As soon as she sat back on her heels, he ran to the makeshift bed and lay down with a little boy giggle. "Me seep here."

"Would you like for me to tell you a story?"

At his nod, she sat on the floor, getting as comfortable as she could. "One day a long time ago, a little boy decided to go hear the new preacher who was coming through his country. His mother didn't want him to go hungry, so she packed him a lunch."

Tommy patted her on the hand. "Are you mine mama?"

Deborah looked down into his large, questioning eyes, and her heart filled with love. She bent forward and kissed the little guy on the temple, brushing his curly dark hair back from his face. She smiled. "Yes, I guess I am your mama. Is that all right with you?"

Tommy nodded with his own sweet smile.

When he didn't say any more, she continued her story of the five loaves and three fishes that Jesus blessed and multiplied. Before she finished, Tommy's long, dark lashes lay on his cheeks. She tucked the cover around him and pulled herself up from the floor.

When Beth went to sleep in the bedroom, Deborah decided she would lie down and rest before she started preparing supper. Taking a quilt and a pillow from her bed, she went back into the sitting room and snuggled down on the sofa.

She thought of Tommy and his determination to follow his father that morning. He was too young to understand the danger of a little boy, not quite three years old, going off alone across the field. Besides the usual dangers, there was always the chance that the bushwhackers Dane had told her about might be nearby. She didn't think an outlaw would bother a little boy, but she'd rather not find out the hard way. Five months ago she had known so little about children. She thought of her own parents and wondered if they had ever been unsure of the right thing to do in raising her and her brother. They always seemed to know just what to say and exactly the right thing to do. At least her father did. She couldn't remember him ever wavering on a decision. Did he make mistakes? Yes. Forcing her to marry Jamison had been a mistake.

Maybe Dane was a mistake, too. Deborah was happier now than she ever remembered being. But she wanted more. She wanted a real marriage with Dane. She wanted his love because, in spite of her resolve to keep her heart out of this marriage, she had fallen in love with her make-believe husband.

She closed her eyes and brought Dane's features to her mind. Surely her father should not have forced her into a love-less marriage. Certainly not with Jamison. But not with Dane, either. Why had he? The answer that had eluded her before became clear as she remembered how firm she'd had to be with Tommy that morning.

Just as she had known what was best for Tommy, so had her father believed he had known what was best for her. He wanted her to marry a Christian, who would care for her and treat her well, so he chose for her.

She thought of her two husbands. Jamison had professed to be a Christian, and her father still believed that he had been. Dane was a true Christian, and maybe in time he would learn to love her. For the first time, she understood that her father's concern for her had prompted his actions. She whispered a prayer for forgiveness of the anger she had carried toward him for so long.

As Deborah relaxed, she felt herself drifting toward sleep when a flutter in her womb brought her eyes wide open. She placed her hand against the small bulge of her stomach and waited. Again the baby moved and she laughed.

&

Several hours later, Dane led Old Dobbin into the barn. He lit the lantern hanging just inside the door and hung it on the nail by the stall so he could see. Then he closed the door against the cold north wind. Barely October and already winter had nudged the warm weather away. He stripped the saddle from his horse and began brushing him down. The barn felt warm after the damp wind had cut across his face and through his coat on the ride in.

While he worked he thought of his warm house and the woman waiting there who had made a home for him and his little ones. She'd probably have Tommy and Beth fed, bathed, and tucked in for the night by now. His own supper would be waiting on the table when he walked through the door. Each night she waited to eat with him when he came in late. He hadn't expected Deborah to seem so much like a wife. In the five months of their marriage, he'd grown used to her, yet he wasn't used to her at all. So many times he caught himself longing to make her truly his wife. When he watched her with the children. When she rocked Beth to sleep and smiled down at the baby with a mother's love shining from her eyes. When she read to Tommy or told him stories then tucked him into bed with a hug and kiss. But most of all, when he remembered their wedding kiss. The thought of her soft lips that were responsive under his haunted him now just as it had since the day of their wedding.

He threw the brush to the side, breaking his train of thought, and reached for the lantern. After checking to be sure everything was secure for the night, he blew out the light and hung it back beside the door, then went to the house.

As he expected, Deborah sat across the table from him as they ate and asked him about his day. She seemed more beautiful tonight than usual. Her eyes shone in the lantern light, and a smile played around the corners of her mouth. He would like nothing better than to take her into his arms and let her know how much he cared for her. He frowned as he realized where his thoughts were leading.

Dane stood, pushing his chair back. "I'll check the doors and head on up to bed, if you don't mind."

He hated the look of confusion on her face. She probably thought he was as bad as her first husband had been.

"That's fine. I imagine you are tired after putting in such a long day." She smiled and started gathering their dirty dishes.

He felt lower than a snake's belly, but he didn't know how to make things right. He couldn't have a real marriage with her. Especially not now. Not now that he cared so much. If she died, he didn't know what he would do. He nodded and without another word turned to go upstairs. At the bottom of the steps he stopped.

"Deborah."

"Yes?" She turned with an expectant light in her eyes, making him feel even worse.

"I thought I'd go to Stockton tomorrow. We still haven't heard from Wesley, and I'd like to send another telegram to see if anything has changed."

She nodded. "I understand. Do you want me to go with you?"

He started to say no but stopped. Just last week he'd heard about a farm that had been raided while the people were gone. He didn't know if the outlaws would bother a woman, but he didn't want to take a chance. He nodded. "You can either go with me or stay with Mom for the day."

A hesitant smile touched her lips as she looked across the room at him, setting Dane's pulse racing. "If you don't mind, may I go with you?"

He nodded, trying to appear as if he didn't care. "Suit yourself. Mom will probably keep the kids so they don't have to make the trip in the cold."

"Yes, I know." Deborah's smile widened. "She asked me Sunday when she could have them for the day. I think she misses them."

"Probably." Dane turned back toward the stairs. "I'll see you in the morning then."

෨

Deborah glanced across at Dane. He sat beside her on the buckboard seat, his eyes straight ahead. He'd been quiet all

morning. When they dropped the kids off with their grandmother, he had scarcely spoken to anyone. Deborah had hurried
to kiss the little ones and tell them to be good before he ushered
her back outside.

A brisk breeze lifted the rim of Deborah's bonnet, and she
huddled closer into the blanket she had pulled around her
shoulders.

"Are you too cold?" Dane's voice startled her.

"No, I'm fine." She smiled at him. "Even my toes are warm."

"Those bricks will be cold on the return trip."

Deborah looked up at the leaden sky that seemed to be
pressing close around them and hoped they would not get
wet before the day was over. "Maybe the sun will come out
and chase the cold away."

Dane smiled for the first time that morning. "Yeah, maybe
so. Stranger things have been known to happen."

Deborah laughed. "You don't believe it will, do you?"

"Nope." The twinkle in his eyes when he slanted a glance at
her let her know that his mood had lifted.

"All right, then. I'll have to pretend all by myself." She looked
ahead and saw the village in the distance. "We're almost there,
aren't we?"

"Just about. I want to go by the telegraph office, and then
we can do some window shopping if you'd like."

"Window shopping?" Deborah couldn't believe he had
suggested such a thing. She hadn't known there was a man alive
who would offer to let her browse through a store. Did he know
how much she missed living near a large city with more stores
than she could visit?

"Sure, that means you can look, but you can't buy."

When he laughed at the shocked look on her face, she
knew he was teasing, and she punched his arm. "Oh, you! Just
for that, I may buy the store out."

"Oh, yeah? I'll be keeping a close eye on you today, then." Dane's chuckle warmed her heart. He didn't laugh nearly enough. She'd like to see him truly happy and wished she could be the one who brought him out of the grief and sadness that seemed to be so much a part of his life.

They rode into town and parked near the courthouse. Deborah went with Dane and waited while he sent his telegram. As he had promised, he took her to a couple of stores and let her look to her heart's content. He even walked through the stores with her, pointing out things that he thought might interest her. He picked out a comb and brush set and against her protests that it cost too much, paid for it, then presented it to her before they left the store. By the time they headed home, Deborah knew that much more of this treatment would send her head-over-heels in love with her husband.

On the way home, Deborah sat as close to Dane as she could without touching him. The cold, damp air made her long for the warmth of their little house. Before they were halfway home the first snow of the season began to fall.

Dane held one hand out and caught a snowflake on his glove. He held it in front of Deborah and watched it melt before looking at her with a serious expression on his face. "I reckon that was some of that sunshine you were talking about on the way to town. Only I never saw white sunshine before, did you?"

"Oh, you!" Deborah shoved her shoulder into his side, and he swung his arm around her in what she assumed was a reflex movement. But he kept his arm there and pulled her close.

Their playful mood dissolved as quickly as the snowflake had disappeared from his glove. He looked down into her eyes. She watched his gaze move across her face and lower to her lips. Without conscious thought she lifted her face toward his as her lashes lowered. When his lips touched hers, they were cold, but warmed within seconds as they lingered, taking and giving from emotions that had been building for the past five months.

Deborah felt as if she had just received her first kiss when Dane pulled back and looked at her with a dazed expression. Never before had she experienced such warmth and love. Then Dane's face grew hard and cold, and she realized she had never before felt so lost and alone when a kiss ended. Dane removed his arm to take up the reins again without a word spoken. He sat, staring straight ahead as if she did not exist. How could he shut her out so completely after sharing such a moment with her?

Snowflakes fell in a silent curtain around them. Deborah pulled the blanket close about her shoulders and watched the cold, white flakes melt on her dark woolen skirt. She knew why Dane had pulled away from her, but knowing didn't stop the hurt. Why was he so afraid of childbirth? Women had babies all the time, some many times. There were several large families who attended the little country church with them. Even his own mother had given birth to seven healthy babies. Why did he think that she would die just because his first wife had? More important, what would he do when he found out she would be giving birth in another four months anyway?

She spread her hand over her rounded abdomen and knew she could not continue much longer to hide her condition. Soon the baby would grow so much that even a cloak would not cover her condition. She was surprised that Cora or one of the women at church hadn't already noticed.

Dane's father came out of the house as soon as they pulled up. "Thought we might be gettin' a snow. Looks like it's stopped now."

"Yeah." Dane started to get down, but Aaron stopped him.

"Mom thought you might as soon leave the little ones here for the night. She's been hankering to have 'em over for a spell now."

Dane looked toward the west. "It's an hour before dark."

"Don't matter to her." Aaron looked from Dane to Deborah and back. "Might jist as well take her up on it. Give ya some time to yourselves."

Deborah felt Dane stiffen, but she didn't look toward him. She couldn't. If his father only knew how things were, he wouldn't suggest they spend any time alone. After a few moments of silence, she knew Dane had given in when he picked up the reins.

"All right. Tell her I'll be after them in the morning."

Aaron nodded and headed back toward the house as they drove off.

Neither spoke the rest of the way home. Deborah knew what Dane was thinking. He didn't want to go home with her without the children to act as a chaperone. His kiss that afternoon had told her that he was attracted to her. But he was afraid. Well, he didn't need to worry. She would keep her distance.

The snow had stopped some time ago, and now the sun made a feeble effort to show itself through the gray blanket of clouds low in the west. Dane stopped the buckboard near the house and helped Deborah climb down.

"I'll be in as soon as I put the buckboard away and take care of Old Dobbin."

"All right." She took the package of candy for the kids and her new comb and brush set. Then, without a backward glance, headed toward the house.

As soon as she stepped inside, she knew something was wrong. Stifling the scream that filled her throat, Deborah turned to run back outside and felt a man's hand close around her arm.

"Not so fast, ma'am." The low voice came from behind her. "Where's your man?"

"What are you doing in my house?" Deborah tried to see the man who held her pulled back against him by both of her arms.

"I asked you where's your man."

"Maybe this will help her talk." A second man stepped out of her bedroom. He pointed a long gun at her. She didn't know what kind it was but thought it looked like the ones the soldiers had carried. Were these men the bushwhackers they'd been hearing about?

The blood drained from her head leaving her dizzy as if she might faint, which was something she had never done before in her life. She fought against the fear that crept over her mind and heart. She couldn't panic now. Dane didn't know anyone was in their house. She had to do something to save him.

twelve

Dane drove the buckboard to the barn. He knew his mother thought she had done them a favor, giving the two of them time to be alone. If she only knew. He thought of Deborah. He should never have given in to the temptation of her sweet lips earlier, but he hadn't been able to stop when she looked up at him. They'd been having fun together, just as if they really were sweethearts. And he'd ruined their day by kissing her. And wanting to kiss her again. If only he could, but he knew that once he got started, he wouldn't be able to stop with a few kisses.

His mind churned with thoughts of Deborah and what they could have if there were no danger of her becoming pregnant. He longed to have a true marriage with her. One where he felt free to love her as a husband should love his wife. Not only physically but emotionally as well. If he had known how hard it would be to keep his emotions in check, he would have never gotten married again.

He stopped in front of the barn and got down to open the doors and saw footprints, not quite covered by snow, in the damp ground. The doors were not latched the way he always left them. He looked at the footprints again. Two men had gone into the barn and then walked toward the house. His heart stopped in his chest. Deborah could be in danger.

How stupid could he be? He knew outlaws had been raiding nearby, and he'd let his wife go into the house alone after they'd been gone all day. Berating himself for his lack of forethought and for becoming so caught up with his own churning emotions, he grabbed his rifle and crept toward the house.

As he rounded the corner, he saw the front door standing open. Keeping to the side where he wouldn't be seen, he moved toward the door, his rifle ready. At the edge of the door he peered in. A man stood with his back to him. His heart froze when he saw that the rifle in the man's hand was trained on Deborah while a second man shoved her into the rocking chair. That was the break Dane needed.

Without waiting to think about Deborah's fear or his anger at the rough treatment she had just received, he took quick aim and fired. With the loud boom from his gun ringing in his ears, he watched the man fall to the floor, clutching his leg. A string of curses flew from his mouth, disgusting Dane. He saw the man with the gun move and reacted by falling back against the cabin's rough log siding just as a ball zinged past his head.

Dane rushed through the open door, his rifle held ready. The other man came at him, and Dane stepped to the side at the last second, bringing the butt of his rifle down hard against the back of the man's head. Momentarily stunned, the outlaw shook his head and turned to fight. Dane again used the hard wood of his rifle in a sharp blow to the man's head, knocking him to the floor. The outlaw's rifle slid out of his reach as he slumped, unconscious near the door. Dane turned, ready to give the injured man some of the same treatment and saw that he still sat on the floor holding his leg while he rocked back and forth, moaning.

"Deborah, are you all right?" Dane kicked the outlaw's rifle toward the center of the room while he reloaded his own rifle.

"Yes, I'm fine. Do you need something to tie them up?"

"You wouldn't happen to have some rope on you?" His attempt at levity met with a wide-eyed look from Deborah.

He knew she was frightened, and he didn't know how to reassure her.

"No, but I started to braid a rug from some old woolen material. Would it work?" Deborah got up and went to the corner where she kept her sewing projects.

"Probably, but I'd hate to cut up your rug." He kept his rifle on the injured man who sat against the wall, scowling at him.

"That's all right. It really isn't very long yet." She handed him a length of braid. He saw her hands tremble at the same time he heard a sound outside.

"Hey, what's going on here?" Billy stuck his head in the door. He came in followed by Lenore.

"We heard shots clear over at our place." Lenore looked from one man to the other. "This one's coming around. What did you do, catch the outlaws everyone's been worrying about?"

"Yeah, I think so." Dane tossed the braid to Billy. "Here, help me get 'em tied up. We'll turn them in tomorrow in Stockton."

Billy held up the woolen braid. "Fancy rope. Okay to cut this?"

"Yes, go ahead." Deborah sat in the rocking chair with her hands clutched in her lap.

Dane felt sorry for her—and proud of her. She'd walked into a nightmare and hadn't fallen apart. Most women would have been hysterical by now.

After they had the men tied and the flesh wound taken care of on the one Dane had shot, they locked them in the empty smokehouse. Dane asked Billy if he'd like to go with him the next morning to the sheriff in Stockton.

"Wouldn't miss it. I'll be over at daylight."

"I'm glad the babies weren't here," Lenore said.

Dane agreed. "God must have put it in Mom's heart to

keep them. They'd have been with Deborah when she went in the house."

He stood outside the smokehouse talking with Billy and Lenore, but he wanted to be in the house with Deborah. He knew she had been frightened, and he needed to see that she was all right.

As soon as his cousins left, he went inside and found Deborah huddled in the rocking chair. Tears ran down her cheeks in silent testimony of her fear.

He knelt in front of her. "Hey, it's all right now. We've got those two tied and locked in so tight they'll never get loose."

A strangled sob escaped her lips, and she leaned forward wrapping her arms around Dane's neck. He held her close, murmuring assuring words while a strong desire to protect and keep her close overwhelmed him, banishing his carefully planned reserve.

He slipped one arm under her knees and, cradling her close, stood to lift her from the chair. She melted against him, her arms wrapping around his neck, her sweetness wrapping around his heart.

She must have surprised the outlaws before they could ransack her bedroom. Both the other rooms had been gone through, as evidenced by the food he'd seen piled on the kitchen table and the clutter of things pulled out. Deborah's house was always neat and clean just as her bedroom was now. He laid her on the bed and took off her shoes. She sat up.

"Do you want me to help you change into your nightgown?"

She shook her head. "I can do it."

When he would have walked out of the room, she reached toward him. "Dane, will you stay for a while?"

Without answering, he moved to the other side of the bed and sat down, keeping his gaze away from her while she changed. He felt the bed dip when she climbed under the covers. He turned to look at her, and she pulled the covers back. "I'm so cold. Can you hold me just until I stop shaking?"

Dane took his shoes off then slipped beneath the covers and stretched his arm under Deborah's head. She scooted close enough for him to feel the trembling in her body. He rubbed tiny circles on her shoulder.

"I don't think you are cold so much as in shock. You'll be fine as soon as you've had a good night's sleep. I'm proud of you, Deborah. You know that?"

She shook her head, and he kissed her forehead. "I am. You stood up to those men just fine. Most women would have screamed or swooned, but you kept your head and even thought of using the braid for a rope."

"I don't know what I'd have done if they'd hurt you. I was so scared. I knew they would kill you if you walked through that door."

"You were scared for me?" Dane had trouble accepting that thought.

She nodded. "Yes, very."

Dane fell silent, marveling at the woman beside him. She was one in a million and he knew it. He did not deserve the sacrifice she had made by marrying him. She deserved so much better than he could ever be. He held her for a long time until the trembling stopped and she fell asleep. He could have eased away from her and gone upstairs to bed, but he couldn't seem to make his muscles obey. Instead he sent a silent prayer heavenward. He thanked God for keeping Deborah safe and for allowing him to hold her now, even if for only one night.

Then he closed his eyes and went to sleep, waking early the next morning to find Deborah snuggled close beside him. Dane lay for a moment absorbing the fact that he had slept next to Deborah for the first time in their five months of marriage. How he wished that things were different so he could make a habit of waking every morning to Deborah's beautiful face. But nothing had changed.

He eased his arm from under her neck, taking care to not wake her. When he was free he picked up his shoes and stood watching her sleep. He hadn't planned to fall in love with Deborah. He'd thought he could marry a woman he didn't know and keep his distance, emotionally and physically. He couldn't imagine life without her.

He thought of Anne and knew he hadn't stopped loving her. But something had changed there, too. In less than a year, the pain of losing Anne had dimmed. Deborah had brought healing to his soul, to the grief he thought would never leave. She had brought life and laughter and even love back into his life. Deborah had found her own place in his heart. He loved her. An overwhelming tide of love swept through him, and he bent across the bed to kiss her on the cheek and on her forehead. He had never before felt so much love for anyone, but with his love came sadness. Deborah could never be fully his.

Dane slipped from the room and closed the door without a sound. He put his shoes on in the kitchen then put the food still on the table back where it belonged. With as little noise as possible, he straightened up the house before going outside to meet Billy.

⁂

When Deborah woke she reached for Dane and found he'd gone. As she came fully awake she sat up and looked at the pillow beside hers. A smile touched her lips when she saw the indention where his head had been. She spread her hand out on the bed where Dane had slept. The covers were still warm. A smile touched her lips. Dane had stayed through the night.

She thought of his gentleness when he held her. He said he was proud of her. She wondered if he might love her a little. After last night, she knew she loved him. Then she remembered the men who had grabbed her, and a shiver coursed down her back. She threw the covers off and ran from her room, hugging herself against the cold chill that would not leave. No one was in the sitting room or the kitchen. She opened the door and looked outside but saw no one in the early morning light.

She turned back to find a square of paper on the kitchen table. Her hand trembled as she picked up the note from Dane and read, "I've gone with Billy to take the outlaws to Stockton. I'll go by and get the kids on my way back. Don't worry about breakfast for us. Just take it easy. You've earned a rest, Dane."

She read the note twice before laying it back down. For a reason she didn't understand, she felt disappointed. She was thankful that those awful men were gone. With no one to cook for, she could laze away the morning. But she felt so alone. The house felt empty and cold even with the stove radiating heat from the fire Dane had built before he left. The warmth she craved was that of Tommy's childish prattle and Beth's baby sounds. But mostly she had wanted to see Dane before he left. To reassure herself that he was all right and that he would still treat her with the tender concern that he had the night before. Would he sleep in her bed again? Had last night marked a change in their relationship, or would he force them back to being strangers living in the same house?

Deborah went to her bedroom and dressed. After she gathered the eggs from the few hens still laying, she spent the rest of the morning cleaning the house and preparing the noon meal for Dane and Tommy.

She took the pan of potatoes off the stove just as she heard the wagon turn in toward the house. She almost dropped the pan on the table in her hurry to get to the door. Grabbing a shawl from the back of a chair, Deborah threw it over her shoulders and ran outside.

Dane drew to a stop when he saw her. His wide smile gave her the assurance she needed that he did care for her. "We got them delivered. Sheriff was mighty happy to take 'em off our hands."

"I'm glad. Did you have any trouble with them on the way?"

Dane shook his head. "No. Billy rode behind with his shotgun trained on them the whole way. They were afraid to move."

"Maybe we can rest easy now with no outlaws taking what isn't nailed down." Deborah leaned over the side of the wagon bed to see Beth. Dane had her so bundled against the cold in her little bed that all Deborah saw was a mound of quilts.

"You want to take Beth? Tommy's going to help me give Old Dobbin some oats."

Deborah smiled at Tommy who sat close to his father on the wagon seat. "So you're a big boy, are you?"

Tommy's big blue eyes, so like his father's, looked seriously at her as he nodded. "Me help."

Dane handed Beth, quilts and all, to Deborah. She smiled at the tiny face of her little daughter that peeked out. "I'll unwrap this package and then you two need to come in for dinner. It's on the table."

As she turned away, a thought occurred to her. "You haven't already eaten, have you?"

Dane grinned. "Nope. Mom tried to get me to, but I figured you'd have something ready."

Deborah smiled. Didn't that prove he cared? She turned away and went inside. As she discarded the covers that had kept Beth warm, she talked and played with the baby and felt as if she and Tommy had been gone forever instead of only twenty-four hours. Beth had grown so much in the last five months. She'd been crawling for some time and had recently started pulling up to the furniture. Soon she'd be walking. Her baby was growing up.

At that moment Deborah felt movement that reminded her of another baby that would soon make an appearance. She placed her hand on the small mound of her stomach and marveled at the new life within. How much longer could she keep her secret from Dane? How much longer did she want to?

She set Beth on the floor to play while she finished setting out their dinner. She put Beth in the high chair and pulled it up to the table just as Dane and Tommy came in the back door.

"Something smells good in here." Dane stopped at the washbasin to wash his and Tommy's hands.

"Probably the bread. I always like the smell of fresh-baked bread."

"Oh boy, Tommy." Dane picked the little boy up and set him in a chair at the table. "Looks like Mama went all out."

Deborah blushed at his praise. His smile held a tenderness she hadn't noticed before. His voice was low with concern. "Are you all right?"

"Yes, I'm fine now."

Dane reached for Tommy's hand and took Beth's little hand in his. Deborah did the same on the other side of the table as Dane bowed his head and offered a brief prayer of thanks for their food.

Before they finished eating, someone pounded on their door. Dane shoved his chair back as Lenore burst into the room. Her eyes were wide, her face splotched from crying, her hair straggling from the bun in back. Mud spotted her dress.

She ran across the room and grabbed Dane's arm, pulling him with her. "Dane, come quick. It's Billy. He fell and I can't get him up."

Without a backward glance, Dane and Lenore ran from the house.

thirteen

A cold November wind dried the ground and left frost on the brown grass in the early morning of Billy Reid's funeral. By midmorning, the sun came out, promising warmth to the shivering mourners that gathered around the open grave in the little cemetery beside the church.

Deborah stood close to Dane. She felt his hurt, knowing that although he hadn't always agreed with Billy, he had loved him. But the worst was Billy's relationship with God. She knew Dane had tried to get Billy and Lenore to go to church with them, but they had always found an excuse. Neither would they listen when he spoke of salvation. Now she could only assume that Billy had not been ready for death, and she felt the weight of that knowledge.

Lenore stood with her parents. Tears ran down her cheeks as great racking sobs shook her body. She held a handkerchief to her eyes and then tore it in her anguish. Deborah had never felt so sorry for anyone in her life as she did Lenore. Surely she must have loved Billy. How terrible that he hadn't known.

Dane had told Deborah that after delivering the outlaws to the sheriff, Billy had taken off across the country alone. They didn't know where he had gone, but when he didn't come home as expected, Lenore had gone looking and found him not far from the house facedown on the ground. His horse had apparently slipped in the mud when he'd tried to jump the creek at its narrowest point. Billy's neck broke when he landed.

Poor Lenore. To have found her husband that way. Deborah

121

wiped her own tears when Billy's mother hugged Lenore, and they clung to each other crying.

Dane and Deborah left as soon as they could get away. Although the children were bundled against the north wind, they didn't want them exposed to the cold too long. Beth, as usual, took their outing without a fuss, but Tommy had been ready to leave long before the service ended. Deborah looked forward to his nap time.

Dane stopped the wagon at the house and helped Deborah carry the little ones inside. He stoked the fire in the cookstove, adding a couple of sticks of wood, then went back outside to care for his horse.

Deborah busied herself with the children and in putting a meal on the table. She fried potatoes and onions with thin-cut strips of cured ham. Reheated beans and cornbread completed their meal. As she filled glasses of milk, Dane came in and helped Tommy wash his hands.

Deborah watched him as she lifted Beth into the high chair. She didn't know what to do to ease his pain. How could she say everything would be all right? How could she bring comfort to him when his cousin might be lost not only to him but to the Lord as well? She said nothing.

After Dane's prayer, Deborah dished out small portions for Beth and Tommy before taking food for herself. She handed Beth a spoon to keep her hands busy while she fed her. She smiled at the baby's attempt to scoop beans up in her spoon. She looked across the table at Dane and shared a smile that didn't reach his eyes.

"She thinks she's all grown up." Deborah slipped a bite of potato into Beth's mouth.

"We spend the first twenty years of our lives trying to be older than we are and the rest wishing we were younger." Dane's voice broke on the last word.

"Yes, I guess that's true."

Dane pushed his chair back, his plate still half full. "I've got work needing done in the barn. If I don't come inside in time for supper, don't wait for me."

"All right." Deborah agreed, although she knew she would set back a plate for him.

She watched Dane put his coat on and go out the back door. Did he want to get away by himself because he grieved for Billy? Or did he want to get away from her? Deborah knew he hurt for Billy and he would for some time to come. But since the night he held her after they caught the outlaws in the house, he had kept his distance, denying the special bonding that had begun between them.

She had so hoped he would continue to share her bed after that one night, but that had not happened. The next day Billy had died, and Dane retreated into the polite stranger he had been before. Maybe she had dreamed the closeness they'd shared. Maybe Dane didn't care for her as she had hoped. But she hadn't dreamed her own feelings. She loved Dane Stark as she had never loved another man. She would love him until she drew her last breath.

When Beth turned away from the spoon and Deborah noticed Tommy's eyelids drooping, she cleaned Beth's hands and face and put her to bed, glad that she was such a docile child. She washed Tommy's face and hands next and went upstairs with him.

"Would you like for me to tell you a story?" She tucked the covers around him and sat on the edge of his bed.

At his nod, she began the story of Jesus's birth but stopped when she saw that he had fallen asleep. She kissed him on the forehead and went downstairs.

By the time Dane came in for supper, the children were again in bed sleeping for the night. Deborah set his plate on the table and poured a glass of milk.

"I ate with the children, but I'd be glad to sit with you while you eat. If you'd like, that is."

"You don't have to." Dane bowed his head in silent prayer then picked up his fork. "Thanks for saving some back for me."

Deborah sat across the table from him and forced a smile. "You are welcome. I know I don't have to sit with you, but I want to. If you don't want me here, you can tell me to leave."

The corners of his lips twitched. "You know I won't do that."

This time she gave him a real smile. "I was hoping you wouldn't."

When he'd eaten in silence for a few minutes, she asked, "So how was your day in the barn?"

He chuckled and she loved the sound. "That makes me sound like an animal."

She laughed softly. "It does, doesn't it? I didn't mean it that way. I just wondered if you got a lot accomplished."

His expression hardened. "Not much. I spent most of the time asking God why He took Billy when he wasn't ready to go. The rest of the time I asked Him why He doesn't send Wesley home."

"Did you get an answer?"

He shook his head. "No."

"I've often heard my father say that God's ways are above our ways. We cannot begin to understand the mind of God. But He is a just and righteous God. We need never fear for He has our best interests in mind."

Dane stared at Deborah until a faint smile touched his lips. "I would argue with that, but I'd be in the wrong. Billy was almost a year older than me. We played together all our lives. And fought. Seems like we always competed for the same things. Trying to outdo the other."

He seemed to be looking into the past. Deborah waited. When he spoke again, moisture filled his eyes.

"But Billy wouldn't ever come to the Lord. Aunt Ivy prayed for him and taught him the right way all his life. He laughed at everything I said. Maybe he would have come later if he'd lived."

Deborah reached across the table to lay her hand on Dane's. "Maybe he wouldn't have. Sounds to me that he knew what was right. You and his mother and probably everyone else did what you could. Don't you see, Dane? It was his choice in the end. Everyone has to decide for themselves whether they will serve the Lord or not."

"I've been racking my brain all afternoon trying to figure out what I could have done—what I could have said that would have made a difference."

"Nothing." Deborah shook her head. "You couldn't have done anything more than you did. God gave us each the will to decide. We can't save people. Only God can do that and then only if they will let Him."

Dane smiled his first real smile that evening. "Thank you. I do feel better, but would you mind praying with me? I'd like to pray for Lenore and Aunt Ivy. I know they are hurting tonight. This hit them pretty hard."

Deborah came around the table and sat in the chair next to Dane. She took his hands in hers and bowed her head. She led in prayer, asking for comfort and peace to each person who loved Billy. She prayed for Dane that he would receive God's assurance and peace in his heart. Then Dane prayed and cried.

Deborah felt tears running down her own cheeks as she heard her husband sob. He held her hands tight so that she could do nothing but sit and pray for him. Finally he grew quiet and released her hands to fumble in his pocket for a handkerchief.

"Again, thank you. I don't think I could have gotten through tonight without you."

Deborah stood. "I'm glad I could help, but I'm sure you would have come to the same conclusion."

"It's late, isn't it?" Dane shoved his chair back and kissed her on the forehead. "Why don't you go on to bed? I'll lock up and bank the fires."

Deborah's heart soared as she turned to her bedroom. Would he come to her bed tonight? She wanted desperately to have a real marriage with Dane. She loved him as she had never believed possible.

She changed into her nightgown and opened the door to receive warmth from the fire. She climbed into bed, pulling the covers up to her chin in the chilly room. She could hear Dane moving about; then she heard his footsteps on the stairs leading to the rooms above, and she knew he would not be coming to her that night. Tears filled her eyes and she dashed them away. Oh, well. If he got too close, he would discover her secret before she was ready.

She spread her hand over her rounded belly and wondered how much longer she could hide her baby. What good would keeping her secret do, anyway? Soon Dane would know, and what would he do when he found out? Would he send her home to St. Louis before she became too big? Would his gentle, caring manner with her turn to anger? She fell asleep with the determination that she would hide her baby as long as she possibly could.

❧

Sunday evening had been set aside as a special service with singing only. When they pulled into the churchyard, Dane asked Deborah, "You are singing tonight, aren't you?"

She laughed. "I've been asked to."

"Then that means you are." He grinned. "Nobody sings as good as my wife."

Deborah felt a blush cover her face. She had never heard him refer to her as his wife before. "Oh, Dane."

"No, I mean it. When you sing, there's not another sound in the church. Nobody wants to miss a single note. I wouldn't be surprised if the angels stopped to listen."

"I think we'd better go in before you have me so nervous I can't sing."

Dane laughed as he came around to help her and the kids.

Another wagon pulled to a stop beside theirs. A family that lived across the creek climbed down. The two sons ran toward the churchyard where other children were gathering.

"You boys better not get dirty," their mother called to them, then turned to Deborah. "You will be singing tonight, won't you?"

Deborah heard Dane's soft chuckle as she nodded. "Yes, Brother Donovan asked me to prepare a song."

"Only one?"

"Maybe two, but that depends on how many others will be singing."

"I'll be hoping for two, then."

Dane carried Tommy while Deborah took Beth, and they followed the other couple to the church. As they greeted others, almost all assured Deborah that they were looking forward to her singing. She sang a special song almost every week. The people were used to hearing her, but they never seemed to get tired of listening to her voice.

She realized as she sat midway in the church beside Dane that she didn't mind being asked to sing anymore. Before, in St. Louis, she had resented having to sing in each service. Was that because her father had given her no choice? Or had she simply been rebellious? Most of her life she had resented the high-handed way her father ruled over her. She had not wanted to marry Dane any more than she had wanted to marry Jamison.

Now she thanked God every day for allowing her to marry Dane. Even with a make-believe marriage, she couldn't imagine her life without Dane and the children. She loved all three as if they had always been her real family.

Brother Donovan opened the service with prayer and a congregational song before the special singing began. Deborah sang near the middle of the service and again toward the end. Although the crowded church felt warm, Deborah kept her long, flowing cloak on when she stood in front of everyone. Her full skirt hid her baby well, but she didn't want to take the chance that someone would notice before she had a chance to tell Dane. And how to tell Dane was a problem she hadn't figured the answer to yet.

At the close of the service, Brother Donovan asked Deborah to sing an invitational song while he called the people forward for prayer. She stood to the side in the front as she sang "Just a Closer Walk with Thee." By the time the song ended, many had come forward to pray. As their voices were raised in prayer, she started again at the beginning and when the song ended the second time, slipped to the back of the church where Cora stood holding Beth.

As soon as she got close, Beth lunged for her, calling, "Mama."

Cora smiled. "I'd say she knows who loves her."

Deborah took her daughter and smiled at her mother-in-law. "I do love her just as if she were my very own. And Tommy, too."

Cora slipped her arm around Deborah and hugged her close. She pulled back with a wide smile. "Oh, my. Is there something you and Dane should be telling us?"

Deborah felt as if the temperature in the building had risen twenty degrees. She looked Cora in the eyes and said, "No, because Dane doesn't know."

Confusion showed in Cora's eyes. "How could he not notice? When do you plan to tell him?"

"I don't know." Deborah put her hand on Cora's arm as if to keep her from running to Dane. "Please don't mention it to anyone until I can tell him."

Cora shook her head. "Deborah, what's going on?"

Deborah looked around and knew that they couldn't talk in confidence for long. "The baby isn't Dane's. It's my first husband's. I didn't know when we got married, but I'm afraid to tell him now."

"Oh." Cora also looked around the church at her friends and neighbors who would soon be filing out past them. "Why?"

Deborah kept her voice as low as she could. "He's afraid of childbirth because of Anne. He doesn't want me to have a baby, and I don't know what he will do when he finds out."

"Oh, Deborah, I'm so sorry." As the import of Deborah's confession hit Cora, her eyes widened and she put a comforting hand on the younger woman's arm. "I had no idea. But you must know that you can't keep a baby hidden under a full skirt and an apron for much longer."

"Yes, I do know. I'll tell him soon. I promise."

"When will it be?"

"I think near Christmas."

Cora nodded and whispered as Brother Donovan prayed a dismissal prayer. "You have remained small so far, but babies blossom in the last three months. The sooner you tell him, he better."

fourteen

With Thanksgiving barely two weeks away, Deborah decided she needed to inventory her supplies. Dane's parents would be providing the turkey, one they had raised especially for this meal, but she wanted to make some pies and contribute a dish or two.

Tommy played quietly on the floor, so Deborah set Beth in her high chair with some spoons to bang while she sorted through the jars of canned goods she had put up through the summer as well as some Anne had left. She pulled green beans and pumpkin out and set them on the table just as Dane burst through the door.

"Wesley's back!" A wide smile lit his face. "Mom sent Benjamin to tell me."

Deborah knew Dane, as well as the rest of his family, had been worried about Wesley. The war had been over since April, and they'd had no word from him in all that time. To have him return now before the holiday season was a special miracle for the entire family.

Dane crossed the room and caught Deborah's shoulders in his hands. His eyes sparkled with happiness, and he drew her ever closer. Deborah's heart caught in her throat. Not only did he intend to kiss her, but also in his excitement, he planned to hold her close. He would without doubt feel the baby who at that moment decided to wake and stretch.

Just as his hands slid across her shoulders to encircle her, there was a quick tap on the door and it opened a second time. Dane stepped back, turning to see who had come in.

Lenore closed the door and turned to face them. Deborah didn't know whether to be glad for the interruption or resent the intrusion.

"Have you heard that Wesley's back?" Dane's smile had not dimmed.

"Wesley's back! That's great news." Lenore seemed as pleased with the news as Dane had been. In fact, she crossed the room to give Dane a hug. "I am so glad to hear that."

Deborah stood to the side and watched Lenore get the hug that should have been hers. *Billy isn't cold in his grave yet, and already she's after my husband.* The thought had no sooner taken form in Deborah's mind than she felt ashamed. Of course Lenore wasn't trying to take Dane from her. Just because Billy thought Dane and Lenore were in love, that didn't make it so. No doubt she missed her husband very much.

"Deborah." Dane brought her attention to him. "I'd like to run over and see Wesley for a few minutes. Then tonight we can all go and spend some time with him and the rest of the family. Mom wants us there for supper. Is that all right with you?"

"Of course. You should go see him." Deborah smiled, pleased he had asked her. "I'll look forward to meeting him tonight."

Dane did something then that surprised her. Right in front of Lenore, he gave her a quick kiss on the lips. She tried to act natural, as if he did such things all the time. Lenore's eyes narrowed as if she suspected Dane was putting on a show for her benefit.

"Me wanna go, too, Daddy." Tommy tugged on Dane's pant leg.

"Grab your coat. It's cold outside." Dane helped his son bundle up with mittens and woolen hat and carried him out.

As the door closed behind them, Lenore took Beth from the high chair then pulled a chair out from the table and sat down with her. She ignored Deborah while she talked and played with the baby. "How's my angel girl?"

Beth's mouth spread in a wide smile as she soaked up the attention. Lenore looked up at Deborah "So what are you doing today?"

Wishing her visitor would go home, Deborah answered, "I thought I would see what I have to cook for Thanksgiving dinner."

"I suppose you'll be eating with the Starks."

"Yes, we will."

"Why do you bother pretending?"

Deborah stared at Lenore. "Pretending what?"

Lenore shrugged. "You and Dane. It's so obvious, everyone knows."

Deborah's hand rested on her stomach. Had she been fooling herself? Cora had noticed, but surely no one else had. Dane still didn't know about the baby.

When she didn't respond, Lenore shook her head. "That kiss. Your marriage. It's all a big deception, isn't it? You can't honestly believe anyone thinks you have a real marriage. You don't even sleep in the same room."

The hot flush of anger swept over Deborah. "What business is it of yours whether our marriage is real or not?"

Lenore shifted Beth to the side. "Because Dane loves me."

Lenore's words were like a cold dash of water, leaving Deborah without breath. She groped for a chair and sank to it before her knees gave way.

"Oh, come now. Don't act so surprised. Dane and I have been in love for years. I got mad at him and married Billy so he married Anne to get even with me."

"Why are you telling me this?" Deborah could barely choke

out the words past the pain in her heart.

Lenore leaned forward. "You don't even have to get a divorce. You've never shared his bed, so you can get an annulment and go back to St. Louis where you belong. Maybe you can find a real husband there. Then Dane will be free to marry me. Anne and Billy are both gone. This is the chance we've longed for all these years."

"How dare you!" Deborah jumped up, shoving her chair back. "You can't come into my house making such claims. If my husband wants a divorce, he will have to ask me himself. And I'm—I'm with child."

As soon as the words were out of her mouth, Deborah wished she could call them back. Everything she had said was true, if misleading. She knew better. Her father had told her often enough to make sure her speech was honest in meaning as well as in words. But before she could make amends, Lenore shoved Beth at her and ran to the bedroom.

"Wait!" Deborah called to her. "You have no right to go into my bedroom."

Lenore ignored her and pushed the door open. She looked around, then headed toward the stairs.

Deborah ran to the foot of the stairs. "Lenore, stop. It's none of your business."

She might as well be speaking a foreign language for all the attention she got. Lenore shoved her way into Tommy and Dane's room.

Deborah could feel her blood boil. "This is not your house or your business." Deborah could hear the words echoing off the walls as she raised her voice at Lenore. How could Lenore do this? What did she think she was going to prove?

Within seconds Lenore came back down the stairs, a triumphant smile on her lips.

"So, you share his bed, do you? I suppose that's why his

things are in one room and yours are in the other. Looks to me like Dane sleeps with Tommy and you sleep with Beth."

Deborah heard the wagon go by the house to the barn. Dane was home and from the way Lenore's eyes lit up she knew it, too. She smiled at Deborah. "You can get the annulment at the courthouse in Stockton. I'll be glad to go with you. How about Thursday?"

"Get out of my house." Deborah jerked the door open and glared at Lenore. She held Beth close in her arms. "Get out and from now on stay away from Dane and our family."

Lenore pulled her coat on as she stepped through the door. "Think about what I said, Deborah. You're too young to be stuck in a pretend marriage with a man who doesn't want you."

Deborah slammed the door and moved to the window as Lenore ran past toward the barn and Dane. She could follow Lenore to the barn and create another scene in front of Dane, but what good would that do? If Dane didn't want her, he wouldn't listen to anything she had to say.

She sat down and rocked Beth, who had been upset by the confrontation with Lenore, until Dane came in with Tommy, barely stepping inside the door before he went back out. Deborah heard him chopping wood just outside the back door and assumed that meant Lenore had gone home.

As the day wore on, her imagination supplied more information about what had gone on in the barn that morning than she wanted to know. She tried to convince herself that Dane would never be unfaithful even if he didn't love her. Dane was an exceptional man. A Christian man. He treated her with respect and kindness. She had never met a gentler man who cared for his children more than Dane did.

Lenore said she and Dane had been in love for many years, even before either of them had married. If so, Dane could still be in love with Lenore.

Deborah wrestled with her thoughts all day. She withdrew, saying little when Dane came inside for the noon meal. He didn't seem to notice as he talked about Wesley. When the war ended, he said, Wesley had decided to go west to see what lay beyond the plains. Dane said he'd gone all the way to California before turning around and coming back home. Deborah thought Dane's brother inconsiderate for causing his family so much worry while he was gallivanting all over the country and beyond, but she kept her opinion to herself since Dane seemed so happy to have him home.

When the children took their naps, she laid down, too, since she wouldn't have to get supper that night. Just before falling asleep, with tears pooling in her eyes, she prayed for wisdom that she would know what to do about Dane and Lenore. Then she prayed for strength to leave Dane and return to her father's house if that should be God's will.

Later, after Dane helped her to the wagon seat and climbed up beside her, he picked up the reins and they started the drive to his folks' house. Neither spoke for the first few minutes, then Dane said, "Are you feeling well, Deborah?"

She swung around to look at him. "Yes, I'm fine."

His gentle smile made her want to cry. "You're awfully quiet. More so than usual. Anything bothering you?"

"Nothing important." When had she taken up lying? Even without meaning to, it seemed she said things that were not completely true. "I mean it wouldn't be important to anyone but me."

"Then it is important." He touched her cheek with his gloved finger, sending waves of love straight to her heart. "Please tell me what it is."

Deborah hesitated. He would think her jealous and he wouldn't be wrong. She decided it didn't matter. If he didn't want her, he could think whatever he wanted. "I saw Lenore go to the barn before she went home."

"Yes, she did. She wants me to go over sometime this week to do some chores for her. With Billy gone, everything has fallen on her shoulders. Her father has been doing what he can, but he's got his own work."

"That's all she wanted?" Deborah searched Dane's eyes, trying to see beyond his words to the truth.

He looked back at her with an open, honest expression and the hint of a smile that warmed her all the way to her heart. "Yep, that was it. You don't mind if I help her out, do you?"

How could she say that she did mind when that would make her look even worse than she felt? She shook her head. "No, that's fine. I'm sure she does need help."

She might want help with chores, but mostly Lenore wanted Dane. This plea for help was a ploy to get him where she could flirt and win his heart again. Deborah could see in Dane's bright blue eyes that he did not know of Lenore's plan. Still, she knew that a man could be easily persuaded to agree with the woman he loved. Soon he would know and then he would be offering to drive Deborah to Stockton himself. Especially when he found out about the coming baby.

At the Starks', Cora took Tommy from Dane and gave her grandson a kiss on the cheek. She took his coat and set him on the floor. As he ran off, she took Dane's coat. "Go visit with your brother."

Levi stepped to Deborah and took Beth, creating a scramble of uncles vying for her attention. "Hey, how's my baby girl?"

"You don't want him. Come see Uncle Ashton." Beth's baby words, coos, and giggles blended with the young men's voices as they settled in the sitting room to play with her.

"Help me carry the wraps into the bedroom, will you, Deborah?" Cora started through the sitting room and Deborah followed.

Cora threw the load she carried on the bed before turning to close the door. "Are you all right? Are you getting enough rest and plenty to eat?"

Deborah smiled and, tossing her coat to the bed, gave Cora a quick hug. "Thank you for being concerned. The answer to both is yes. I take a nap with the children almost every day." She patted her tummy. "And, from the looks of this, I'm getting plenty to eat."

"Have you told Dane?"

Deborah's smile disappeared. "No."

Cora's gaze rested on the barely discernable mound under Deborah's full, flowing skirt. "I will admit you are hiding it well, but you must know that he will take the news better if you tell him."

"I promise I will."

Cora smiled. "Come and meet Wesley. All seven of my boys are home tonight. We have much to be thankful for." She slipped an arm around Deborah's shoulders. "We have a full house of sons, a daughter, and two—almost three grandchildren. God is so good to us."

When Deborah met Wesley, she felt as if Billy had come back to life. Beyond the physical resemblance, he had the same cocky grin and lazy assurance of a son much loved. When Lenore showed up at the door without escort, Deborah's heart sank. She didn't feel up to facing her adversary, but Lenore paid little attention to either her or Dane.

She threw her arms around Wesley and the two embraced almost as if they were lovers.

"I heard about Billy." Wesley pulled back and looked at Lenore. "If there's anything I can do, jist give a holler."

Still cuddled in his embrace, Lenore looked up at him from under her lashes. "Well, since you mentioned it—I could use a big, strong man to help me finish bringing in wood for the winter. Billy never did get around to getting it all done."

"Sounds like fun, long as you're there, too." Wesley released her and sat back in his chair. Lenore plopped to the floor beside him.

Deborah realized there weren't enough seats for everyone without bringing chairs from the kitchen, but she felt embarrassed by the way Lenore clung to Wesley and the way he soaked up her attention. Maybe he felt sorry for her. Maybe she was glad to see him. And maybe she didn't care as much for Dane as she let on. Dane didn't seem to notice, but he could be hiding his feelings. Deborah didn't know what to think and was glad when Dane said it was time to go home.

"Lenore, would you like to ride home with us since we're going your way?"

Wesley took Lenore's arm. "No way, big brother. I'm taking her home. Right, Lenore?"

Lenore looked from Dane to Wesley with a flirtatious expression. "Right, Wesley." She turned back to Dane, but her gaze shifted to Deborah. "You don't mind, do you, Dane?"

Dane shook his head. "No, of course not."

Deborah looked at Dane to see if he really did care, but he was helping Tommy with his coat. He either didn't care or he was doing a good job of covering his feelings. She felt so confused inside. She didn't know what to believe.

fifteen

The following Sunday morning after church Deborah stopped to speak to the preacher's wife, and when she turned around, Dane had gone outside. A rare warm day in late November, everyone soaked up the sun while they could. Children played tag, running among and around the adults. Deborah stood on the porch steps with Beth wrapped in a warm blanket. She shaded her eyes against the bright sun as she looked from one group to another trying to see Dane.

Then she saw him. With Lenore. They stood to the side alone. Their heads were together as in a deep discussion. Deborah's heart sank. She had hoped that Lenore would turn her attentions to Wesley, but that didn't seem to be happening.

Deborah turned her back on her husband and joined Cora who had Tommy's hand securely in hers.

&

Dane had let Tommy pull him outside when Deborah stopped to talk to Sister Donovan. Then Lenore had latched on to his arm, and Tommy ran across the yard to his grandmother. When he saw that Tommy was all right, he turned to see what Lenore wanted.

"I need to talk to you." She pulled him away from the others.

"What's the matter?"

"There's something I think you need to know." Lenore looked around as if afraid someone might overhear. "Has Deborah told you about the baby?"

"Beth?" His heart missed a beat. "What about her?"

"No, not Beth. I'm talking about Deborah's baby."

Dane frowned. "What are you talking about?"

A satisfied smile set on Lenore's face. "I see she hasn't told you. Open your eyes, Dane. Deborah is with child. Probably by her first husband. Don't worry; I know the baby isn't yours."

Dane stared at Lenore. Surely she was wrong. She laughed, and he knew she had just made him confess that he and Deborah had not lived together as husband and wife. They had been married over six months. A real husband would know if his wife were with child in all that time. How had she hidden a baby from him for so long?

He looked across the yard at Deborah. All the women wore fluffed-out skirts that would hide anything, he supposed, even a baby. But six months? Or would she be seven months along now? He intended to have some answers. Without another word, he turned away and met Wesley coming to take possession of Lenore.

"Hey, Dane," Wesley greeted him.

Dane gave him a curt nod, never taking his eyes from Deborah.

"What's the matter with him?" he heard Wesley ask then Lenore's laughing response as Dane walked away.

"Oh, just a domestic problem. Don't worry about Dane. I'd rather talk about Wesley. Why don't you tell me some more about your exciting trip into the Wild West?"

Dane touched Deborah's elbow. "Are you ready to go home?"

She smiled up at him and his heart melted. She was so beautiful. So pure and innocent. Lenore had to be wrong. Surely, Deborah wouldn't have deceived him. She knew how he felt about childbirth. But, of course, that was the problem, wasn't it? She knew and—and what? Was afraid to tell him? Thought she could keep it a secret? Hardly. A woman could not keep the birth of her child a secret from her husband. To keep the unborn child a secret for six months was feat enough.

Dane did not speak on the trip home. He stopped near the house and helped Deborah take the children inside, and then he went to the barn. He took care of Old Dobbin and the buckboard. He paced from one end of the barn to the other, picking up a harness and hanging it, moving tools, and doing nothing worthwhile.

With each minute that passed he thought of Deborah. He remembered their wedding day when she walked down the church aisle toward him. That was when he had really seen her for the first time. When he'd realized how lovely she was both inside and out. He should have called off the wedding. But he couldn't. He hadn't wanted to.

He sank to the milking stool and buried his face in his hands. That was when he'd started falling in love with Deborah. And each day for the last six months she had taken a small piece of his heart until now she had it all.

Lifting his face to the rafters and beyond, he cried out, "Lord, help me. I can't lose Deborah, too."

He stood then and went inside to the warm meal Deborah had waiting on the table.

After they ate, Dane took Tommy upstairs for his nap. He read a story to him, tucked him in, and gave him a kiss. Then he went downstairs to confront Deborah.

She stepped out of her bedroom as he reached the lower floor. "Deborah, could we go into the kitchen?"

"Of course." Her eyes were large and questioning, but she followed him.

He held her chair and sat across the table from her. Deciding the direct approach would be best, he looked at her and asked, "Are you with child?"

Her hands moved to caress her stomach, but she held his gaze. "Yes, I am."

"When will the baby be born?"

"Near Christmas."

"Did you honestly think you could hide it from me forever?"

She shook her head, her eyes closing for a moment before she looked back at him. "No, but I was afraid to tell you."

"Why?"

Instead of answering, she asked, "Will you send me away?"

"Of course not." He towered over her. "Is that why you married me? Because of the baby?"

She shrank against the chair. "No. Honest, Dane, I didn't know about the baby until after we were married." Tears glistened in her eyes. "I'm sorry. I really didn't know."

He glared at her, angry and hurt. One tear slid down her cheek and another followed. She didn't move, but sat with her hands protectively hiding her child and watched him while she cried. He wasn't angry with her. In his mind he knew she hadn't done anything wrong. But deep within he felt as if she had tricked him somehow. He had kept himself from her. No matter how much he had wanted a normal relationship with her, he had been strong so that this wouldn't happen. Yet, it had happened in spite of his sacrifice.

He couldn't watch his wife go through childbirth. He couldn't stand by while she screamed until she could scream no more. He couldn't kiss her cold, pale lips for the last time and hear the echo of dirt hitting her casket for the rest of his life. He just couldn't. Not again.

He stumbled toward the back door and jerked it open. He heard her call his name just before he closed the door.

❧

Fresh tears blurred Deborah's eyes. He hated her. He said he wouldn't send her away, but he might as well. He would never love her. Not after she had hurt him so much. She turned and buried her face in her arms on the table, letting the tears flow as she prayed for Dane and for God's direction.

After a long time, Deborah rose and moved to the couch in the sitting room where she lay down, letting the hurt in her heart settle into a dull ache. She closed her eyes and slept, waking to the stirring of the children. Her head ached and her eyes felt swollen. Her body seemed big and heavy and her lower back hurt, but she got up and spent the rest of the day with Tommy and Beth.

She fixed supper, but Dane didn't return to the house so she fed the children and let them play until bedtime. After the house grew quiet, she stood at the window looking out into the dark night. Where had Dane gone? To Lenore? No, she didn't think he would do that. Their marriage wasn't real, but she knew he would be faithful even to a pretend marriage.

She tried to think where he might have gone, but she couldn't imagine him taking their problems to anyone else. She turned the lamp down low and stayed up to wait for him. The room grew cold, so she added wood to the fire, then curled up on the couch under a quilt.

❧

When Deborah opened her eyes, sunshine streamed across the couch. She sat up as the previous night's vigil returned to her mind. She threw the covers off and went upstairs. Tommy lay asleep on his bed. Dane's covers were rumpled, but he was gone.

Deborah let her breath out and realized she had been afraid that he hadn't come in at all. She went back downstairs to fix breakfast. Surely he would come in to eat.

Dane did come in. He spoke to Deborah as if nothing had happened. Then after they ate, he ignored her. He roughhoused with Tommy and tickled Beth until both children begged him to stay and play with them. Beth had progressed to walking as long as she could touch something solid. If Dane moved out of her reach, she dropped to the floor and crawled to him.

He picked her up and held her high above his head, bringing baby giggles and squeals. Deborah smiled as she watched them. Dane was a wonderful father. His children loved him without fear. That was something she had never known and desperately wanted for her own unborn child. If only Dane could love her as much as she loved him. If only he could accept her child as his, just as she had accepted his children.

But Dane didn't love her. He pulled some hard candy from his pocket and handed one to each child, kissed them, and told them he had to go to work. Then he turned to Deborah.

"Don't worry about lunch for me. I've got a lot to do today."

In November? Deborah didn't ask what he would be doing. She wondered if he even knew. Obviously he planned to keep his distance.

The weather turned cold, and still Dane found so much outside work that he spent little time in the house with Deborah. On Thanksgiving Day, she wondered if he would find something else to do so that they wouldn't have to pretend at his folks' house. But he became a polite stranger just as he had been when they were first married.

He carried her offerings of two pumpkin pies and a couple of vegetable dishes out to the wagon. He helped bundle the children against the cold and helped her climb into the wagon.

They hadn't been with his family long before Cora took Deborah aside. "What's wrong, Deborah? Did you tell Dane?"

"Lenore told him."

Cora's eyes widened, but she didn't comment on that. "He's just worried then."

"Maybe."

"Of course that's it. What else could it be?"

Yes, what else, indeed? *Unless Lenore is right that he is in love with her. He'd probably like for our marriage to be annulled.* Deborah knew Dane would never ask. She almost wished he would. She didn't know how much longer she could stand being ignored by the man she had grown to love so much.

Deborah woke Friday morning with another headache. Her lower back ached constantly, and she could find no comfortable position for sleep. She had spent most of the night thinking of Dane and Lenore. Billy and Lenore had both said that Dane was in love with Lenore. She had known Dane such a short time. She hadn't expected to fall in love with him, but she had. She loved him so much that she would sacrifice her own life for his if necessary. It would be such a small thing to give him the annulment he wanted.

She knew her decision was as selfish as it was sacrificial. Dane didn't love her and he never would. He thought she had deceived him by marrying him while she carried a child he did not want. She could not continue to live in the same house with a man who despised her. And she would not subject her child to a lifetime of neglect by a father who doted on his own children. She was sure Dane would never abuse her child, but neither would he treat an unwanted child the same as his own children.

Deborah dressed and fixed breakfast. When Dane came in to eat, she asked him to hitch the wagon for her. "I'd like to go to your mother's."

"We were there just yesterday."

"I know. I didn't get a chance to really talk with her, though."

"Deborah, you can't drive a wagon in your condition."

"I'm fine."

"No, I'll take you later this afternoon and you can visit all you want. You can wait."

Deborah watched Dane go to the barn. He came out a

few minutes later, leading his saddle horse. That meant Old Dobbin was still in the barn. Deborah went into her bedroom and packed a bag. She'd like to take everything but knew she could never lift a trunk into the wagon. She straightened the house, working as quickly as she could.

The last few weeks she had been feeling the burden of her body, as the baby seemed to be growing all at once to make up for staying so small the first few months. She had awakened that morning with a strange feeling and knew if she didn't go to Stockton today, she might not have time before the baby was born. When she was sure Dane was gone, she wrapped the children against the cold and carried Beth while Tommy walked.

With the children sitting in the back of the wagon, Deborah got the harness for Old Dobbin. She had been so confident that she could hitch the horse to the wagon without a problem. But that was not to be. Dane made the job look easy, when in reality, the harness weighed almost more than Deborah could lift.

By the time Old Dobbin stood in place, she felt as if she had done three days' worth of laundry all rolled into one. Sweat poured from her face and body. Her breath came in quick puffs of vapor that drifted away in the cold air. A pain moved through her body so that she gasped and bent double. When it went away she straightened. She climbed onto the wagon, feeling awkward and heavy. Her head pounded until she wished she could go back inside and rest. Instead she settled Tommy and Beth in the little bed with covers tucked around them.

She picked up the reins and shook them as she'd seen Dane do. Old Dobbin stepped out and they were on their way. Halfway to the Starks', another pain ripped through Deborah's body, bending her forward with her hands pressed against her rounded stomach. She took short, quick breaths until the pain eased.

What had she done? Dane said she couldn't drive the wagon in her condition. He had been afraid she would hurt herself. Fear for her baby's life crept through her heart. She should have listened to Dane. By hitching the horse to the wagon she had killed her baby.

"Haw!" she called to Old Dobbin to hurry. He picked up his pace and she felt the warmth of her water break. Tears ran down her cheeks as she realized the foolishness of her actions. Dane would be so angry with her. If her baby died she wanted to die, too. She sagged with relief when she saw the Starks' cabin appear.

Old Dobbin stopped in front of the house, and Cora came outside as if she had been expecting them. She rushed to the wagon. "Deborah, what's wrong?"

"My baby." Deborah burst into tears. She heard Cora issuing orders as another pain ripped through her body, and then strong arms lifted her from the wagon seat and carried her into the warmth of Cora's house.

sixteen

Dane rode across the pasture, his mind on Deborah while he searched for the missing cow and calf. He'd been so worried about his problems at home that he hadn't realized he had a cow ready to give birth. If he'd had his mind on his job, he'd have brought her in to the barn so he could keep an eye on things and make sure they were all right. But he'd let it go and now she was off hiding someplace in a vain attempt to protect her young. Oh well, cows generally went through the birthing without a problem. On the other hand, humans didn't always fair so well.

He rode on looking behind every tree and in every clump of brush he passed, determined to spend the day away from the house and the fear he felt every time he looked at Deborah. The fear that he would lose her. He loved her more than he'd ever dreamed possible. He couldn't imagine living without her.

He thought of the child she carried—of the fact that her child was not his. Could he raise another man's child? The jealousy he had denied from the time he knew of the baby's existence surrounded him like an ugly fog. If his wife must go through childbirth, he wanted the baby to be his. And he wanted them both to live. He lifted his eyes to the gray-covered sky and prayed for Deborah and her baby.

The soft cry of a baby calf caught his attention, and he swerved toward the sound. He found mother and baby without a hitch and soon had the calf across the saddle in front of him with his mama trailing behind. They made it to the barn before Dane saw his father walking toward him.

His lifted his hand in greeting. "Hey, what's up?"

"Deborah's at our house."

Dane swung from the saddle then carried the newborn calf into the barn where he established mother and baby in a stall. He called over his shoulder, "How'd you all know she wanted to go to your place? I told her I'd take her this afternoon."

Aaron hurried after his son. "Dane, you'd best listen. She hitched the wagon and come on her own."

Dane swung around and stared at his father. "She what? Is she all right?"

Aaron shook his head, his expression guarded. "Your mom says the baby was comin' anyhow, but I don't reckon hitchin' a wagon helped none."

"Dad, please." Dane grabbed his father's arms. "Is Deborah alive?"

Aaron nodded. "She was. Now are you comin'?"

"Of course." Dane left his father to close the barn as he ran to his waiting mount and set out in a run to Deborah, his heart racing faster than the horse.

He left his horse with Levi and ran inside. The door to the bedroom just off the sitting room was closed. Benjamin sat at the kitchen table. No one else was around. Dane headed toward his younger brother.

"What's going on? Is she—" He couldn't get the rest of his sentence out past the tightening in his throat.

"Naw, she's all right. Mom says the baby's just comin' early. Mrs. Newkirk's in there with them. I'm supposed to wait out here in case they need something." He looked up at Dane with a hopeful expression. "Since you're here now, can I go?"

Dane scarcely registered what his brother had said except that Deborah was all right. He nodded. "Sure, go on."

As soon as the door closed on Benjamin, Dane started praying. He prayed while he paced across the floor from the kitchen to the door that shielded him from Deborah and back to the kitchen. Over and over he made the trip alone until his father came inside.

"Anything happen yet?" Aaron pulled a chair out from the kitchen table and sat down.

Dane sat next to him and shook his head. "I don't know what's going on. I'm afraid I'll lose her, Dad, and I don't know if I could go through that again."

"They say birthin' babies is natural. But every time your mom went through it I vowed that'd be the last one. 'Specially with the twins. I couldn't handle the worry and the fear no more."

"But you did. Six times."

Aaron nodded. "She wanted you, ever' one. Anne always was frail. Deborah's like your mom. She'll do fine."

"She's early, though. Anne went until her time and still didn't make it. I don't know what I'd do if. . ." He looked away, closing his eyes against the thought.

"You love this girl?"

Dane turned and met his father's concerned gaze. "It's different than it was with Anne. I thought I loved Anne, but I don't know anymore. Deborah is so vital, so much a part of my life in so short a time. When I get near her I want to touch her, to make sure she's really there and that's she's mine. I never felt that way with Anne."

"What about the baby?"

Dane knew what his father was asking, but he didn't have the answer. "I don't know. I haven't had time to get used to the idea. I don't know if I can be a father to someone else's child."

Aaron stayed with Dane until Cora came out and prepared lunch. The rest of the family ate, but Dane mostly pushed his food around. He realized Tommy and Beth were there, and then Cora took them upstairs for their naps. The house grew quiet, and his mother went back into the bedroom. After what seemed like hours, he heard Deborah cry out and he heard the tiny cry of a baby; then he didn't hear anything more. He sank to the kitchen table and prayed.

"Dane, you can go in and see Deborah." He hadn't heard his mother come out of the bedroom.

"Is Deborah. . . ?"

"She's fine. Go on and let her know you're here."

Dane stood on shaky legs and crossed the sitting room to the open door. He stepped inside the room and stood staring down at Deborah. She lay in the bed with her eyes closed. She didn't look fine to him. As he watched, Mrs. Newkirk took the blanket bundle from Deborah's arms and she didn't move.

"Would you like to see the baby?" The midwife stepped to him. "She's early so we've got to keep her warm, but she's strong. I'll put her in a box on the oven door."

"The oven?" Dane looked at the tiny face framed by the blanket. The baby's eyes were closed, too. Would either of them live?

"Yes, the oven will keep her warm until she adjusts to the air in the house. I'll stay at least until tomorrow so we can make sure she's all right." She pulled the blanket back over the baby's face. "You have a fine daughter here, Dane. Why don't you sit with Deborah awhile? She's tired, but she'll wake up if you talk to her."

Dane looked back at Deborah as Mrs. Newkirk went out the door. She hadn't moved. He couldn't see her breathe. They would both die—Deborah and her baby. He turned away as panic rose in his chest, choking him. He couldn't stay and watch her die.

As he ran out the front door, Cora came from the kitchen. "Dane, what's the matter?"

She called to him, but he didn't stop. He heard her behind him. "Dane, wait. Deborah's all right."

He stopped. "She's going to die, Mom. Just like Anne did. I tried to keep this from happening. Why? Why did God do this to me? Why did He give me a woman to love then jerk her away from me in the very same way He took Anne? I know it was my fault Anne died, but not Deborah. I stayed away from her, Mom. That baby isn't mine." A sob shook his frame. "I was afraid I'd lose her, so I kept away and it didn't matter."

Tears ran down his cheeks and sobs shook his shoulders as he turned from Cora and hugged his arms in front of his chest. Grief, even more intense than what he had felt for Anne, held him in its powerful grip.

Cora's arms went around her son, and she held him close. He clung to her and cried until he could cry no more. He pulled away first. "I'm going home, but I'll come back for the kids."

"Dane, look at me." Cora touched his cheek, forcing him to meet her gaze. "Deborah is not dying. She's tired, that's all. Let her sleep and build back her strength. When she's well, take her home and love her. Don't be afraid to make her your wife in every way. I can't promise you that Deborah will live to be old any more than you can promise Deborah that you will. We didn't expect Billy to die, did we? Death is part of life. But you can't let your fears take the joy out of living. Please promise me you will love Deborah and you will treat her baby just as if she were your very own."

Dane looked away. "I don't know if—"

"Dane, there's one thing more." Cora waited until he looked at her. "I know you blame yourself for Anne's death. You don't have to answer me, but think about this. What did Anne have to say about Beth? She knew the risk after she had such a hard time with Tommy. Did you force her to have another baby, or did she want to?"

Dane looked at the ground so he didn't have to see the compassion in his mother's eyes. "I'll think about what you've said. Please take good care of Deborah. I love her, Mom. Even more than I loved Anne. I know that now. Anne will always be a part of my past, and I did love her. But if Deborah dies, I don't think I can go on."

Cora smiled. "I understand more than you know. I feel the same way about your father. But the older we get, the more I realize it's going to happen someday whether I want it to or not. One of us will go first. So I've decided to live each day as the gift that it is from God. Enjoy Deborah's love while you have her with you. Don't ask for trouble, Dane."

Dane didn't make any promises as he turned toward the barn. He'd find his horse and go home where he could spend some time in prayer. He felt as if he'd been hit with a boulder and he wasn't sure where he might fall.

That evening when Dane returned for his wagon and his children, Cora pushed him into the bedroom. "Deborah's awake and she wants to see you."

He hadn't been sure what to expect, so when he saw Deborah propped up in bed with color in her cheeks and a shy smile for him, he felt a heavy burden roll from his shoulders. He stood by the door. "How're you doin'?"

"I'm fine." Her smile disappeared as she clutched the quilts in front of her. "I wanted to tell you that I'm sorry I took the wagon."

"Yeah, it wasn't too good an idea. You could have killed yourself." He realized he was still a little sore at her for taking such a risk.

"Your mother and Mrs. Newkirk both said the baby was coming, anyway. I just hurried things along."

He shrugged. "Yeah, well I came by to get the kids. I'll take 'em home and put 'em to bed."

He wanted to leave. He felt as if he wouldn't be able to breathe if he stood there looking at her another minute. He turned toward the door. "I'll get out of here and let you rest."

Dane was at home and had the little ones in bed sound asleep before he realized he hadn't seen Deborah's baby that night. For the next week Dane fell into his former pattern of dropping the children off each morning with his mother and picking them up at night. He ate breakfast and supper with his folks so he didn't have to cook except at noon. He stopped in for a minute or two each evening to see how Deborah was and saw the baby a couple of times, but he kept his distance for the most part.

During the day he worked hard. Every night after Tommy and Beth went to sleep, he knelt in front of the couch in the sitting room with his Bible and tried to make sense of his life.

Midway through the first week that Deborah was gone, Lenore stopped by at noon to see Dane. "I heard that Deborah had her baby."

He nodded.

"How's she doing?"

"You could go see her."

Lenore shrugged. "Maybe I will. So how are you getting along with her gone?"

"I'm fine, Lenore." He didn't have time to visit with anyone and especially not Lenore. When they were kids she'd followed him around getting on his nerves. She hadn't changed much as an adult.

"Is she going through with the annulment?" Lenore took off her scarf and twirled it through her fingers.

Dane turned from the stove to stare at her, the taste of fear in his mouth. "Annulment? What are you talking about?"

seventeen

Lenore smiled. "I see she didn't have time to tell you. I imagine she was heading to Stockton the day she had the baby. You'll have to ask her if you want to know for sure. All I know is that she was talking about getting your marriage annulled so she could go back to St. Louis and find someone she could have a real marriage with."

Dane staggered under the pain of Lenore's revelation. Had Deborah confided in her? Told her things that she couldn't tell him? He hadn't considered that Deborah might want to leave—hadn't thought beyond his own desire to keep her with him always.

"I had thought about offering to step in and take her place." Lenore walked close and placed a hand on Dane's arm. She smiled up at him. "I don't like living alone."

When he cringed from her touch and stepped back, she laughed and turned toward the door. With her hand on the knob, she looked back at him. "Don't worry, Dane. That was before Wesley showed up. Your little brother can be a lot of fun, you know." With that she swept out, letting the door close on her laughter.

Dane closed his eyes against the hurt Lenore's words had inflicted. He loved Deborah. Why would she want to leave him? Yet, why would she want to stay? He offered her nothing more than a home to clean, children to care for, meals to prepare, and laundry to keep up. What woman would enter a loveless marriage willingly? What woman would stay with a man who withheld his love from her?

Obviously Deborah didn't plan to stay.

Not wanting to confront the continual turmoil that churned through his mind, he shoved the leftover stew to the pie safe and grabbed his coat. He had work to do.

る

For two weeks Deborah stayed with her in-laws while her body healed and her baby filled out, losing the shrunken, wrinkled skin and look of an early baby. She thanked God that little Clara Elizabeth had survived. Dane had scarcely looked at the baby and he spoke to Deborah only when he had to, so she hadn't asked his opinion on Clara's name. She decided she didn't care whether he liked it or not. Just as she had feared, he seemed determined to ignore both her and the baby.

"Mama, is her mine baby?" Tommy pressed against her side while she sat in the rocking chair. He held a finger out to Clara's tiny hand and laughed when she jerked in response.

Deborah held the baby in one arm while she hugged Tommy. She didn't know how to answer his question. Was the baby going to be his sister, or would his father send her away? She decided no answer would be best.

"She's precious, isn't she?"

"Yes." Tommy nodded. "I like babies."

"Let's take her home, then." Dane's voice startled Deborah. She hadn't heard anyone come in.

"Dada." Beth stepped away from the chair she had pulled up to and stopped. She looked up at Dane with her special baby smile.

Deborah held her breath and watched as Dane squatted with his hands outstretched toward his daughter encouraging her. "Come on, Beth. You can do it."

Beth took another step and teetered. She took another, more sure this time. Two more steps and she landed safely in her father's arms. He laughed and picked her up high above his head. She chortled and drooled, barely missing his face.

Deborah laughed. "I think she's cutting teeth."

"I'd say you are right." Dane brought Beth back for a hug. "Were those her first steps?"

"Yes, that was her first without holding on."

"Good girl." Dane hugged her again. "What say we take Mama and go home? Where's Grandma?"

Deborah bit back disappointment that he still ignored Clara. When they got home, she would ask him for the annulment. She knew he wanted a housekeeper and a mother for his children, but surely he wouldn't want her now that he could have Lenore. The children loved Lenore and wouldn't miss Deborah, no matter how much she would miss them.

She forced her thoughts to the present. "She's in the kitchen, I think."

Dane took Beth into the next room. Tommy followed so Deborah took Clara into the bedroom she had been using and packed her few belongings. She had missed her home and even if she couldn't stay long, she was eager to see how Dane had kept the house. When Dane and Cora came back to the sitting room, Deborah was ready to go.

"There's no need for Tommy and Beth to go home tonight, is there?" Cora held her hands out, and Beth fell into her embrace. "Dane, I think Deborah needs your attention her first night back at home. We can keep this big boy and girl one night, can't we?"

Tommy grinned up at his grandma. "Me big boy."

"Yes, you are. Would you like to stay with Grandma and Grandpa tonight?"

He nodded and Deborah held her breath. She loved Tommy and Beth, but she'd very much like to talk to Dane without worrying about them interrupting.

When Dane looked at her and nodded, she released her

breath. He turned to his mother. "If you're sure it isn't too much trouble."

"No trouble at all. Get your things and get out of here. Deborah needs her rest."

Deborah laughed. "I'm fine, really. All I've been doing for the past two weeks is rest. Now it's time I made myself useful."

Before Deborah knew what he had in mind, Dane bent, hooked an arm behind her knees, and picked her up. She clutched Clara close and looked at him with wide eyes.

"What do you think you are doing?"

He grinned at her. "What's it look like? I'm carrying you and your baby out to the wagon. I'll come back and get your things."

"Bye-bye, Mama." Tommy watched them with a solemn expression.

"Bye, sweetheart," Deborah answered. "I'll see you in the morning, all right?"

He nodded and Beth puckered, squirming in her grandmother's arms. "Mama."

"I think now would be a good time for you to get Deborah out of here." Cora turned toward the kitchen, trying to distract Beth.

Deborah heard the little girl's wails as Dane carried her outside. "Maybe we should just take Beth."

"She'll be fine."

Deborah sensed a change in Dane as soon as they were alone. Gone were the grins and light tone to his voice. He set her on the wagon seat and stepped back. "I'll just be a minute."

Dane couldn't have picked a better day for her homecoming. Although the air felt cold against her face, the sun shone down on her head, giving her a feeling of warmth. She had wrapped Clara so that no breeze could touch her; still she held her close, shielding her with her coat.

"Was that everything? Just what you had sitting by the door?" Dane lifted her bag into the back and climbed on.

"Yes, that was it."

They didn't speak again until they got home. Dane stopped by the front door and carried Deborah into the house.

"Dane, I can walk."

"Maybe so, but you don't have to." He took her to the couch and set her in a reclining position against a pillow.

"I'm not an invalid." Deborah didn't know whether to laugh or be angry.

"Sit still. I'm going to get you a hot cup of cocoa." He went into the kitchen and since she sat with her back to him, she kept quiet.

Why was he waiting on her, treating her as if she were a delicate piece of china that might break? She slipped her arms free of her coat and took the outer blanket from her baby. Clara stretched and her eyebrows lifted, but she did not awaken. Deborah looked down at her, amazed at the perfection of each miniature feature. She gently pressed her finger into the tiny open hand and smiled as Clara's fingers tightened around hers. She brought Clara's hand to her lips, then kissed her daughter's forehead. As always when she looked at the miracle in her arms, maternal love overwhelmed her. God had been so good to her.

"What did you name her?" Dane knelt beside Deborah with a steaming cup of cocoa in his hand.

"Clara Elizabeth."

"What about her last name?"

Deborah didn't know how to answer. So much depended on Dane. If she offered him an annulment, would he grab the chance to be rid of her and Clara? She had wanted to talk to him, but now that the opportunity presented itself, she didn't know how to begin. As she tried to form the correct words, she saw a piece of fabric that she didn't recognize draped across the back of the sofa.

"What is that?" She pointed and Dane reached for the fabric.

As he pulled it toward him a strange look crossed his face. The pain of betrayal and jealousy ripped through Deborah's heart. Lenore had been there while she was gone. How could Dane do such a thing to her?

"It belongs to Lenore, doesn't it?"

"Yes." He tossed the scarf to the end of the sofa. "She came by to ask about you. To see how you were doing."

"Why didn't she come to see me? I'd have been glad to tell her myself." Deborah fought against tears that threatened to show Dane how much he had hurt her.

"She said she might. I thought maybe she did."

Deborah looked down at the baby who still slept, unaware of the tension surrounding them. She hated the thought of leaving Dane and the children, but she didn't know what else to do. She loved him so much. She would not—she could not stay here while he loved another woman. It wasn't as if their marriage was real. Dane obviously didn't care.

She looked up and met Dane's gaze. "Lenore didn't come to see me. Several women from the church came at different times. The pastor and his wife came. Everyone thinks Clara is a beautiful little girl."

"Deborah, you didn't tell me about her last name."

"I don't know. That depends. I thought maybe you would want to go with me to Stockton and have our marriage annulled. I don't guess there's much reason to give her your name if we aren't married."

Dane pulled back. "No, I guess not."

He stood, his expression guarded as he looked down at the baby. When he finally spoke there was a sneer in his voice.

"Well, Clara Elizabeth Asberry, it's been nice meeting you. I hope you have a life filled with love and get a new father who will spoil you just as much as you deserve."

Deborah sat watching him, not understanding. She had thought he would be relieved to have her step out of the way. Instead he acted as if she had hurt his feelings.

"Does that mean you want the annulment?" She hoped with all her heart he would say no.

He shrugged. "Why not? That's where you were heading when she was born, isn't it?"

Deborah nodded and watched with a broken heart as Dane turned and walked through the kitchen and out the back door.

eighteen

Dane couldn't stay in the house another minute. He felt as if he might explode if he heard the word annulment one more time. He headed for refuge in the barn. The setting sun sent a rosy glow over the sky, and Dane wondered how God's creation could continue in so much beauty while his life had turned to ashes. He stepped into the warmth of the barn and closed the door. He lit the lantern and hung it on the wall out of the way. He paced from one end of the barn to the other, ignoring the curious stares of the animals.

Lenore had been right. Deborah did want out. She wanted freedom to return to St. Louis where she could find love with a man who wasn't afraid to take her as his wife. And why wouldn't she want that? He couldn't blame her. No normal woman would take on the job he had offered Deborah.

Why had he thought she would be content to serve as housekeeper and substitute mother when all he offered in return was room and board? Not that he believed for a minute that she loved him and wanted his love. No, the missing piece to the puzzle of their lives was the one thing he had taken out of their marriage. The one thing he knew that Deborah wanted: family. She wanted a home of her own. A place where she could love and be loved and know that she belonged. By making their marriage a business arrangement he had denied Deborah the family she craved. And now he had lost her.

The thought of his life without her sent him to his knees in the straw-littered floor. "Lord, please help me. I can't lose Deborah, too."

He prayed while sobs shook his strong shoulders. He asked God to show him what to do—to help him keep Deborah. He thought of Anne and of her death. He couldn't go through that again. Maybe it would be better to let Deborah go than to keep her and eventually kill her in childbirth.

His mother's words came back to his mind. *"What did Anne say about having Beth? Did you force her to have another baby, or did she want to?"*

He remembered the day Anne came to him, telling him that she was going to have another baby. He'd told her then that he didn't want her to go through childbirth again. He was afraid for her life because she'd had such a hard time with Tommy.

Anne had just smiled at him. "I want this baby, Dane. I know you are afraid, but this is a precious life, given by God. I'm not afraid of death. Please don't worry about me. If God calls me home, I will have at least given life to our precious child. God holds my life in His hands. He alone appoints the time when He will take me home. Always remember I wanted another baby. Whatever happens will be all right."

Anne's faith had been strong even though her body was weak. She never could have hitched Old Dobbin to the wagon and driven it the way Deborah had. For the first time Dane compared the two women he had loved and found that they were very different. Anne's strength had been in her spirit. Her will. She had been sickly as a child and had been raised by doting parents to expect everyone to give in to her.

Deborah, on the other hand, had been raised by a domineering father who expected her immediate obedience. No matter how difficult the task, Deborah knew she must bow her own wishes to another. Yet she was strong in body and in spirit. Hadn't she proved that in the hard work she performed every day? She had stood up to the outlaws in her house without a single scream, staying strong until the danger passed. And she had given birth after hitching a wagon and had brought forth a beautiful little girl.

Dane didn't know what to think about Deborah's request for an annulment. Did she really want it, or did she think he wanted it? He bowed again, praying for forgiveness. He prayed that God would help him forgive himself for his part in Anne's death. He asked for a chance to show Deborah how much he loved her. He asked for forgiveness for not trusting God to take care of Deborah. He prayed while tears of regret and repentance wet his cheeks.

≈

Deborah stared at the back door after Dane left while her heart broke. Lenore was right. Dane wanted his freedom so he could marry the woman he loved.

She carried Clara in to Beth's bed and laid her on her back. While she covered her, tucking her in securely, her mind stayed on Dane. She thought of his reaction to her suggestion that they get an annulment. Letting the scene go through her mind again, she remembered the lack of expression on his face when she first mentioned going to Stockton. Why hadn't he seemed happy about her offer of freedom? Why had he taken so long to answer?

Deborah bowed her head. "Lord, help me. Show me the truth. I love him, Lord. I don't want to lose Dane. If there's any hope, if there's any chance that he wants me for his wife, I want to stay."

She returned to the sitting room and kitchen. The house had grown dark. It felt cold and empty with Dane not there just as her heart felt cold and empty without his love.

Deep inside she knew Dane was not happy about the annulment. He didn't want it any more than she did. She stood with her arms crossed staring out the back window toward the barn.

He was out there, she knew. He hid in the barn when he didn't want to face her. Well, he couldn't hide from her tonight. With determination she hadn't known she possessed, she grabbed her coat and looked in on Clara.

"Be good, little girl, while I go get your daddy. It's about time he and I have a long talk. I've decided if I have to fight Lenore for Dane's love, I will. If we're going to be a family, we need to start doing things the right way."

With more bravado than she felt, Deborah hurried out to the barn. She slipped inside, letting the door close behind her without a sound. Dane knelt on the floor to the side and didn't seem to know she was there as he prayed and cried. She couldn't understand what he said, but she knew he hurt and she hurt for him.

She knelt beside him and, placing her hand in the center of his back, leaned against him. He turned toward her and enclosed her in his strong arms. Without saying anything, he clung to her and held her close while sobs shook his body. They stayed on their knees, holding each other and crying until he all at once jerked away.

"Deborah, what are you doing out here? You are supposed to be lying down."

She laughed. "No, I'm not. How can I convince you that I'm perfectly all right? Certainly well able to walk."

He brushed her hair back from her face while his thumb dried the tears on her cheek. "I don't want anything to happen to you. I thought I had lost you when Dad said you hitched the horse up to the wagon and drove yourself to their house. Don't ever do anything like that again. When I saw you lying there in the bed, you looked—"

"I know." She smiled. "I'd just had a busy day. I was tired."

His smile looked so tender. So full of love. "Let's get you back inside."

He stood and picked her up as if she weighed nothing. With long strides he carried her to the lantern. "Could I get you to blow that out?"

She did and hung it back on the hook. He carried her out the door and across the yard then through the kitchen door and back to the couch. "Where's the baby?"

"In Beth's bed." She caught his hand when he started to step away. "Please sit beside me."

When he did, she curled up against him, and he put his arm around her. She turned to look up into his face. "Dane, I want you to understand that I really am all right."

He smiled. "I know that you are."

Deborah felt the wonder of his words sweep through her soul. Dane was no longer afraid. She looked deep into his bright blue eyes and saw what she had longed to see for so long. Dane wanted their marriage to be real, too, because he loved her just as she loved him. She moved closer, and he claimed her lips for his own.

When they pulled apart, Deborah took the crumpled scarf from the end of the couch where Dane had tossed it earlier. She held it up and looked at it. "Lenore told me that you loved her. She said you had loved her for years, but you'd had a fight so she married Billy. She said you married Anne to get even with her."

Dane snorted. "And you believed her."

She looked at him and nodded. "Yes, I had no reason not to."

He shook his head. "She lied. I never loved her. Besides, Anne and I were married first."

"I'm sorry. I had forgotten that both you and Billy told me that. Lenore said I should do the right thing and get an annulment so the two of you could get married. Tommy and Beth love her. I knew they would be all right with her, so what else could I do?"

"I love you, Deborah. I think I started to lose my heart right after Brother Donovan pronounced us husband and wife."

"That was the first time you kissed me."

Dane grinned. "Yeah. I didn't expect to enjoy kissing you so much."

Deborah felt heat rise in her face. "I liked it, too."

"Can we start over, Deborah? Will you be my wife for real?"

"That depends." Deborah held up Lenore's scarf. "What are we going to do about this?"

Dane looked across the room at the fireplace. "Let's burn it as a symbol that we will never let anyone come between us again."

"An excellent idea." Deborah scrambled from the sofa. "Let's do that now."

Before Dane caught up to her, a knock sounded on the front door and it opened. Lenore stepped inside followed by Wesley. Dane slipped his arm around Deborah's waist.

She glanced up at him and smiled, then turned to Lenore as Dane asked, "What brings you out tonight?"

Lenore smiled at him, ignoring Deborah. "We wanted to tell you our news. And, of course, make sure Deborah got home all right."

Deborah spread her skirt out to each side and curtsied. "As you can see, I'm quite fine. I appreciate your concern, Lenore, especially since I didn't realize you cared so much." She held the scarf out. "Oh, by the way, I believe you left this here one day while I was gone."

Dane snickered behind her, and Lenore's face turned red as she snatched the scarf. Wesley laughed. "You got a live one this time, big brother."

Dane pulled Deborah back against his side and smiled down at her. "Yeah, and I hope she never changes." He looked at his brother. "Now what's this news you have to tell us?"

"Reckon I'm gonna try my hand at the married life. Lenore's agreed to go out West with me." He draped an arm around Lenore's shoulders.

Deborah was not overly surprised at Wesley's news, but she was pleased. With Lenore married, she wouldn't have to worry about her trying to steal Dane away. She was so thrilled with the idea of Lenore and Wesley getting married that the full import of Wesley's news didn't hit her until Dane asked, "What do you mean by out West? You aren't heading away again, are you?"

Wesley grinned. "Reckon so. There're great opportunities out in the territories. Land free for the taking. Kind of like our grandpas did here thirty years ago."

"In the Indian territories, you mean."

Wesley shrugged. "There's bound to be some Indians around. Uncle Ben and Uncle Lenny live with the Indians and have for years. I reckon I can get along with 'em, too."

"Our uncles are missionaries to the Indians. What's Mom and Dad say about your plans?"

"Haven't told them yet." Wesley grinned. "Hey, we'll stay until after Christmas and break it to them then. Lenore thought you'd want to know."

"I'm glad you told us and I wish you the best with your marriage, but I wish you'd stay around here, Wesley."

"The war changed us all, Dane. You know that. I can't stay here anymore, but I'll do my best to come back from time to time for visits. Lenore will want to see her folks, too." Wesley eased Lenore toward the door. "Reckon we'll head on out. We'll let you know when the wedding is so you can get us a gift. How's that?"

Dane chuckled. "You haven't changed as much as you think, Wesley."

Lenore stopped at the door and turned to face Deborah.

"I hope there's no hard feelings."

"None at all." Deborah smiled at Lenore. "Without your help, Lenore, I'm not sure Dane and I would have ever found out how much we love each other."

Lenore looked at Dane, her expression sad. "Yes, I think you would have."

Dane closed the door behind Wesley and Lenore then turned toward Deborah as a tiny cry came from the bedroom. Dane grinned. "Our youngest is calling."

Deborah stared at him and then smiled. "Yes, she is. I'll go get her."

"No, you don't. Sit down and rest. I'll bring her to you."

Deborah sat on the sofa, leaving room for Dane. He came back carrying the small baby who had stopped crying as soon as he picked her up. He dwarfed the tiny baby, yet held her with such tenderness in his expression that tears sprang to Deborah's eyes. She had never known such joy existed.

He sat beside Deborah but did not relinquish the baby. He smiled at her wide-eyed inspection of him. "Hey, little Clara. I didn't know you had such pretty eyes. Just like your mama's."

"Mrs. Newkirk said she would sleep most of the time for the first few weeks until she catches up with herself. She was early, after all."

"Yeah, it can't be easy for her." Dane lifted Clara's tiny hand with one finger that seemed huge by comparison. "I've forgotten how little a newborn is."

Deborah smiled. "She's even smaller than most. According to the women I've talked to, we are blessed that she's alive. Most early babies don't make it."

"What about that last name now?" Dane's grin held a touch of uncertainty. "Clara Elizabeth Stark sounds awfully nice to me."

Deborah leaned her head against his shoulder. She loved

him so much. She no longer feared that he would ignore Clara. Something special had happened earlier that night. God had touched Dane in the barn, taking his intense fear away. She'd sensed it when he carried her back inside. Yet she needed to hear the words.

"I think so, too, but before I make it official, I need to know how you feel about a little sister or brother for our three older children."

A ragged sigh left Dane's lungs. "There must have been some prayers going up for me this last year. God met my need, Deborah. I don't guess I'll ever be real comfortable with the idea of childbirth, but more than anything, I'd like for us to have a baby that belongs to both of us."

Clara's face scrunched moments before she let out a tiny wail. Dane handed her to her mother and laughed. "I wasn't asking you, little Miss Stark. I'd rather have your mother's opinion."

Deborah took her baby and slanted a mischievous smile toward Dane. "I think at least two or three more should be about right."

She laughed at his dubious expression then sobered. "But Tommy and Beth already feel like mine."

Dane's gaze shifted to Clara, who was busy making her demands known. He smiled. "Yeah, now I understand that. I think our daughter is hungry. How about you feed her while I fix some supper for us?"

Dane took time to kiss Deborah thoroughly then drop a light kiss on Clara's head before going to the kitchen. While Clara nursed, Deborah watched the love of her life cook—a task she had thought no man would ever do in her presence. But Dane Stark was no ordinary man. She bowed her head for a quick prayer of thanksgiving. God had turned her tears into laughter with a promise of more joy to come.

A Letter To Our Readers

Dear Reader:

In order that we might better contribute to your reading enjoyment, we would appreciate your taking a few minutes to respond to the following questions. We welcome your comments and read each form and letter we receive. When completed, please return to the following:

Fiction Editor
Heartsong Presents
PO Box 719
Uhrichsville, Ohio 44683

1. Did you enjoy reading *Deborah* by Mildred Colvin?
   ❑ Very much! I would like to see more books by this author!
   ❑ Moderately. I would have enjoyed it more if

   _____

   _____

   _____

2. Are you a member of **Heartsong Presents**? ❑ Yes ❑ No
   If no, where did you purchase this book? _____

   _____

3. How would you rate, on a scale from 1 (poor) to 5 (superior), the cover design? _____

4. On a scale from 1 (poor) to 10 (superior), please rate the following elements.

   ____ Heroine   ____ Plot
   ____ Hero   ____ Inspirational theme
   ____ Setting   ____ Secondary characters

5. These characters were special because? _____

_____

_____

6. How has this book inspired your life? _____

_____

_____

7. What settings would you like to see covered in future
   Heartsong Presents books? _____

_____

_____

8. What are some inspirational themes you would like to see
   treated in future books? _____

_____

_____

9. Would you be interested in reading other **Heartsong
   Presents** titles? ❑ Yes ❑ No

10. Please check your age range:
    ❑ Under 18   ❑ 18-24
    ❑ 25-34   ❑ 35-45
    ❑ 46-55   ❑ Over 55

Name _____

Occupation _____

Address _____

City, State, Zip _____

OREGON *Brides*

3 stories in 1

Experience nineteenth-century Oregon with three young women as they learn to love while letting go of the demons of their pasts.

Titles by author Tracey Bateman include: *But for Grace, Everlasting Hope*, and *Beside Still Waters*.

Historical, paperback, 352 pages, 5³/₁₆" x 8"

Heart♥ng

HEARTSONG PRESENTS TITLES AVAILABLE NOW:

Presents

HEARTSONG PRESENTS

If you love Christian romance…

$10.99

You'll love Heartsong Presents' inspiring and faith-filled romances by today's very best Christian authors. . .DiAnn Mills, Wanda E. Brunstetter, and Yvonne Lehman, to mention a few!

When you join Heartsong Presents, you'll enjoy four brand-new, mass market, 176-page books—two contemporary and two historical—that will build you up in your faith when you discover God's role in every relationship you read about!

Mass Market 176 Pages

Imagine. . .four new romances every four weeks—with men and women like you who long to meet the one God has chosen as the love of their lives…all for the low price of $10.99 postpaid.

To join, simply visit www.heartsong presents.com or complete the coupon below and mail it to the address provided.

✂ -

YES! Sign me up for Heartsong!

**NEW MEMBERSHIPS WILL BE SHIPPED IMMEDIATELY!
Send no money now.** We'll bill you only $10.99 postpaid with your first shipment of four books. Or for faster action, call 1-740-922-7280.

NAME _____

ADDRESS_____

CITY_____ STATE _____ ZIP _____

**MAIL TO: HEARTSONG PRESENTS, P.O. Box 721, Uhrichsville, Ohio 44683
or sign up at WWW.HEARTSONGPRESENTS.COM**